THE COLOMBIAN MULE

Massimo Carlotto

THE COLOMBIAN MULE

*Translated from the Italian
by Christopher Woodall*

Europa
editions

Europa Editions
214 West 29th Street
New York, N.Y. 10001
www.europaeditions.com
info@europaeditions.com

Copyright © 2001 by Edizioni E/O
First Publication 2013 by Europa Editions

Translation by Christopher Woodall
Original title: *Il corriere colombiano*
Translation copyright © 2013 by Europa Editions

Library of Congress Cataloging in Publication Data is available
ISBN 978-1-60945-135-6

Carlotto, Massimo
The Colombian Mule

Book design by Emanuele Ragnisco
www.mekkanografici.com

Cover illustration by Emanuele Ragnisco and Marco Flore

Prepress by Grafica Punto Print – Rome

Printed in the USA

THE COLOMBIAN
MULE

Somehow the Colombian knew he was fucked the moment he met the cop's gaze. He recognized that look. He had seen it a thousand times on the streets of Bogotá. It was that special look cops reserved for suspects just before they stopped them. He glanced around.

The other passengers from the Air France Paris–Venice flight were hanging around the carousel, chattering among themselves, joking and laughing. Just like genuine tourists. In a crowd of 150 people, the cop had singled out his face as the one that didn't fit. The intuition of a true professional. The Colombian cast a sidelong glance at the cop and saw he was still staring at him. A bolt of panic shot into the pit of his stomach, crammed as it was with cocaine: pure, Colombian cocaine, the best on the market.

He swore beneath his breath. He had been told there was no need to worry. That entering Italy, landing at Venice, was a breeze. That at Christmas, it was a cinch. The airport would be crawling with tourists and the cops would be too well stuffed with lasagna and panettone to bother chasing mules with bellies full of coke. That's what he had been told. So on Christmas Day he had caught the flight out of Bogotá, changed planes and passports in Paris and arrived in Venice on Boxing Day. When, supposedly, the cops would still be digesting.

The cop winked at his colleagues in the customs box and motioned with his chin towards the Colombian, just to jack up the tension in the mule's guts. They were all staring at him now.

Despite his efforts to smother it, a spasm of fear flashed across his face. He was breaking into a sweat, just a fine film on his forehead and upper lip. Precisely what the cops expected of him.

The Colombian beat off an impulse to make a run for it and forced himself to stay calm. The only way out was through the security gates and onto the runways. He wouldn't make it a hundred meters before they snatched him. He took a deep breath. Then another. Hell, there was no way they could know he was a drug runner; maybe all they wanted was to check his passport. The coke was well stashed. It had taken him the best part of an hour to swallow the pellets—he had made them good and tough so they would withstand the cabin pressure. He didn't want them exploding mid-flight, killing him somewhere over the Atlantic, didn't want to go the same way as Christobal, that poor son of a bitch from the same Bogotá barrio.

The baggage arrived and the passengers formed a neat line. The sniffer dog walked around a few suitcases looking bored. Nobody got stopped. No, it was him the cops were waiting for.

'Passport, please,' asked the one behind the glass.

The mule handed over a passport that had once belonged to a careless Spanish tourist. Until, that is, a couple of velvety-fingered Colombians had brushed up against him on a bus. The cop behind the glass glanced at the document then handed it to the one who had been staring at the mule all along. A smile of satisfaction crept across his face. Anyone could see the photo had been switched. This South-American-looking guy had aroused his suspicions from the start. You could smell he was a drug mule a mile off. In the two years he had been working at Venice airport, he must have seen forty or fifty of them come through. For 2000 dollars, they set off, their guts stuffed with coke, convinced that all they had to do to pass as tourists was put on their only decent suit.

The cop signaled to the Colombian to follow, and led him

into a room full of smoke and men in uniforms. They sat him down and surrounded him.

'That passport's a fake and you're a drug runner,' the cop said in a mix of Italian and Spanish. 'Where are you keeping the coke? In your bags or your belly?' He poked at the mule with his index finger, aiming just above his navel.

The mule looked at the cops' faces and saw there was no way out. 'Aquí,' he answered, pointing at his stomach.

'Colombian?'

'Sí.'

'Who were you delivering it to?'

The Colombian removed one of his shoes and tore off a strip of tape that had been holding a piece of paper folded in four under the heel.

The cop opened it out. 'Pensione Zodiaco, Via Bafile 117, Jesolo.'

Three of the cops then started yelling at the mule, demanding he tell them who he had been taking the drugs to. They wanted to squeeze the most out of the moment. The Colombian shrugged his shoulders and explained that there was a room booked in his name. He was supposed to go there, expel the pellets, and wait for the Italian he had met in Bogotá, the one who had recruited him. He had said his name was Antonio. He had never given his surname. He was about fifty, medium-height, a bit fat, with light brown hair.

A plainclothes cop who had been in the background now snapped his fingers. 'Panierello, call Captain Annetta at the Guardia di Finanza and tell him I'm on my way over. Then see that this gentleman is escorted to the Jesolo Commissariat. I want him kept nice and close to where the meet's supposed to take place.' He moved in closer to the Colombian. 'What's your real name?'

'Guillermo Arías Cuevas,' the mule replied promptly.

'How old are you?'

'Twenty-eight.'

'Where are you from?'

'Bogotá.'

The cop gave him a playful tap on the cheek. 'Well done, kid. You didn't waste our time. The court will take that into consideration.'

Arías Cuevas stared at the cop and shook his head. The son of a bitch was insulting him. It wasn't to grease up to any court that he had decided to cooperate. And it sure as hell wasn't prison that scared him. It was La Tía, that pussy-eating aunt of his. She was going to be more than a little pissed when she discovered he had taken off with 800 grams of her coke.

Opening his door, Ruben Páez found himself standing face to face with Aurelio Uribe Barragán, also known as 'Alacrán', the scorpion, for the lightning speed with which he worked a knife. He was the head of La Tía's gang of killers. As soon as Ruben saw La Tía and her latest lover standing alongside Alacrán, he knew something had gone wrong. The plan that he and Guillermo had put together to make some extra cash must have gone wrong.

'Aren't you going to ask us in, Ruben?' asked La Tía politely—a touch too politely for someone who ran a drug trafficking operation.

La Tía and her girlfriend settled themselves on the bed, the only soft place in the rat's nest of a apartment that Ruben would have done anything to escape—even if it meant ripping off the boss.

La Tía lit a cigarette. There was a time when she had been known as Señora Rosa, Rosa Gonzales Cuevas. Then Guillermo, her sister's eldest, had come along and started calling her Tía, auntie. And everyone had joined in.

She opened her French designer handbag and extracted a flat plastic bottle of Blanco, a low-grade rum that tasted of aniseed. She could have afforded more sophisticated liquor but had drunk Blanco all her life and would touch nothing else. It was a family thing. For generations in the Cauca valley her people had grown the sugar cane used in Blanco. She unscrewed the cap, took a long pull and handed the bottle to the girl, then surveyed the dark red varnish on her long fingernails.

'My contacts in the police have informed me that that punk nephew of mine has got himself arrested in Italy, at Venice airport to be precise, carrying a fair bit of coke. It wouldn't happen to be my coke, would it? Which right now you and Guillermo were supposed to be distributing?'

As though in a conjuring trick, a long special-forces dagger appeared in Alacrán's left hand.

'I don't know, I swear it. I swear on my mother,' Ruben said, staring at the blade. But he gave himself away by pissing in his pants.

Aisa, La Tía's lover, burst into giggles, then smothered her mouth with a chubby hand. She wasn't much to look at and La Tía had had a lot better, but this one was a real rubia, blonde between her legs too, just the way La Tía liked them.

La Tía's tone of voice was unchanged. 'You're too scared to lie, Ruben. It's in your interest to talk. If you like, you can pin all the blame on Guillermo. I don't like my employees trying to rip me off.'

Ruben had no desire whatever to test the sharpness of Alacrán's blade, so he told La Tía how in September Guillermo had met an Italian at Señora Sayago's establishment. He had gone there to drop off the usual consignment of coke and as always had hung around as long as possible. Señora Sayago's was the most exclusive whorehouse in town: the girls were beautiful, the champagne was French and the sheets were changed after every john.

The Italian had come looking for a girl to take with him to Pleasure City, Tokyo's red-light district. They got to talking and when the Italian had found out that Guillermo was La Tía's nephew, he made him a business proposition. It sounded straightforward and lucrative. All he had to do was take a little coke off his aunt, smuggle it into Italy and sell it to the Italian.

The difference in the price of coke in Colombia and Europe would go straight into Guillermo's pocket while the rest of the money would return to La Tía, who would never know the difference. Guillermo had it in mind to do the trip two or three times a year, making thirty or forty thousand dollars on each run. Enough to set him up on his own, make him a name among the narcos. This was Guillermo's first run and he had decided to take advantage of the fact that it was Christmas.

Ruben licked his dry lips. He reckoned he had told it pretty well. He had skated over his own involvement and failed to mention how Guillermo had presented himself to the Italian as a big-time trafficker. He hoped La Tía had swallowed it.

But Rosa Gonzales Cuevas hadn't got to the top of a world dominated by ruthless machos by falling for the kind of stories that little boys like Ruben made up. She was a survivor from the Medellin cartel, which had been defeated at the end of a bloody war by the Cali cartel, which had then gained the backing of the new government and the Yanks. Following the death of Pablo Escobar, La Tía had fled to Bogotá with 400,000 dollars belonging to the organization. It had been just enough to put her back in business, hire some killers and find a blonde chick pretty enough to be seen on her arm. 'Do you know who the Italian is?' asked La Tía.

'No. I've never seen him,' said Ruben.

'You got nothing else to say to me? Maybe that you were in it too?'

Ruben shook his head. La Tía took Aisa's hand, stood up and made for the door. Alacrán stayed behind and slit the boy's throat, using one of those left-to-right slashes that had made him famous throughout Guayabetal when, as an army NCO, he had dealt with peasants who supported the guerrillas.

The lawyer was slim and smartly dressed. He removed his gloves and overcoat, keeping his scarf around his neck. His name was Renato Bonotto. I had worked for him before. He paid well and liked to win. His latest case had to be something pretty big to make him come looking for me during the last weekend of the Christmas vacation.

'What are you drinking?' he asked, pointing at my glass.

I looked at his manicured index finger. 'Seven parts Calvados to three of Drambuie,' I replied. 'A lot of ice and a slice of green apple to chew on once I've emptied the glass. It's called an Alligator and was invented by a barman in Cagliari, to add a little joy to my life.'

'A bit too strong for me. I'm not much of a drinker,' the lawyer said, ordering a port.

I noticed his cell phone. 'Doesn't happen to be GSM, does it?' I asked.

'Uh-huh.'

'Better hand it to the girl,' I said, nodding at Virna to come over.

Bonotto stared at me in surprise.

'It seems the police can listen in on people via their cell phones. Provided they know your number, obviously. You might as well be wired.'

'I can switch it off.'

'Well, that's just the point, you can't. It goes on transmitting, even when turned off. You have to remove the battery and card if you want to disable it. We'll keep it for you at the bar. It's simpler.'

'What is this, the latest urban myth?'

'It seems it's true. Anyway, there's no point risking it. In fact, you ought to consider banning cell phones from your office.'

The lawyer tasted his port.

'I'm acting on behalf of Nazzareno Corradi,' he began. 'He was arrested about ten days ago, the twenty-sixth of December to be exact. I'm going to need some help to get him out of jail.'

'What's the indictment?'

'International trafficking in narcotics.'

'What variety?'

'Cocaine. Eight hundred grams.'

I lit a cigarette. 'Tricky,' I remarked. 'These days the judges are cracking down.'

'At sixty, the chances are he'll die inside.'

I looked Bonotto in the eye. 'You've never defended a drug trafficker so I take it you're convinced your client's innocent. Besides, if you weren't convinced, you wouldn't be here. Everybody knows I don't work for drug dealers.'

'Corradi's clean,' Bonotto reassured me. 'I've known him for years. He used to be a thief, banks, but, on account of his age, he has now turned exclusively to smuggling works of art.'

I checked my glass and settled back, ready for a long and convoluted story. 'So how did he get mixed up with coke?'

The lawyer scratched at his immaculately shaven cheek. I could smell his expensive aftershave.

'At two in the morning, Corradi received a phone call. He was with friends in Treviso, at their place, playing a friendly game of poker. A voice he didn't recognize informed him that his woman, Victoria Rodriguez Gomez, a Colombian, was in room thirty-seven of the Pensione Zodiaco in Jesolo, where a friend of hers was staying, and that she had been taken ill.

Corradi tried to reach her on her cell phone but kept getting a user unavailable message. He jumped in his car and raced to the hotel. There was no one at the desk so he went straight up to the first floor. But when he knocked on the door, a guy with a moustache and slicked-back hair opened up and yelled at him in Spanish to run for it. My client decided he had better find the night porter, but just as he turned round police leapt out from every corner and arrested him.

'The guy in the room turned out to be a Colombian by the name of Guillermo Arías Cuevas. He had been stopped at five o'clock that evening as he came through Venice airport with eight hundred grams of coke in his belly. He had cooperated with the police at once, giving them the address of the hotel, but the description he gave of the Italian who had contacted him in Colombia didn't match Corradi. The statement described a man of about fifty, medium-height, thick-set and with light brown hair, whereas my client is ten years older, almost totally bald, taller and thinner.'

I shrugged my shoulders. 'It doesn't mean a thing. Maybe the Colombian lied. I've never yet met a snitch who told the truth.'

The lawyer threw his arms out wide. 'Either way, my client fell into a trap. He thought he was going to pick up his woman but instead ran into a bunch of cops who are now accusing him of being the mule's Italian contact.'

'So where was his woman?'

'In a lap-dance joint in Eraclea, visiting her girlfriends. It's where she and Corradi first got acquainted.'

'Why did she have her cell phone switched off ?'

'She didn't. The joint's in a basement. There's no signal.'

I motioned to Virna to bring me another drink. 'What have they got on him?'

'Just the fact that he knocked on the mule's door.'

'Well, if you think about it, that's quite a lot. What does the judge make of Corradi's protestation of innocence?'

'He doesn't buy it. He spelled it out for me. Even setting aside my client's previous offences, the fact that he has a relationship with a Colombian dancer and that they have made numerous trips to Bogotá to visit her parents makes it really unlikely that he was at the hotel by coincidence or mistake.'

'What about the phone call that lured him to the trap?'

'It was made from a callbox in Mestre. The judge and investigators take the view that as a lead it isn't even worth looking into.'

'What of the friends he was playing poker with? They must have overheard the conversation.'

'They're all ex-cons with records as long as your arm.'

'What's the judge like?'

'Pisano. A good man. He's open to argument and respects the defense's right to a fair trial. He might seem like the ideal judge. The thing is he has no particular interest in investigation. He just goes along with whatever the police hand him. He'll probably wait for a while and then pass the case on up the line.'

'Then it looks like your client's fucked,' I remarked.

'If he goes to the preliminary hearing with nothing but what we've got right now, then yes, he's fucked for sure. Nowadays trials in Italy are won or lost at the investigation stage. By the time they go to trial, it's too late. You're his only hope of not dying behind bars.'

'I don't see quite what I'm supposed to do.'

'My client is the fall guy in some kind of conspiracy. We need to find out who set him up and why.'

'Have you any firm leads?'

'Just a feeling. Arías Cuevas was initially arrested by Venice airport cops. But then the special narcotics units of both the police and the Guardia di Finanza suddenly piled in. That's really unusual for what was, basically, a low-level operation. Added to that, it turns out that the police were acting under the command of Commissario Nunziante, a sworn enemy of my client ever since that jeweler's store robbery in Caorle.'

'Remind me.'

'There was some shooting, two cops were killed and Corradi was indicted. At the trial I managed to get him off, pleading insufficient evidence. But Nunziante swore to take revenge.'

I took a cigarette out and played with it a bit before lighting it. 'You were right to call it just a feeling. It's not much to go on. Besides, as the man said, there are too many Colombian coincidences.'

Bonotto gave me a worried look.

'You're not telling me you're refusing the case . . .'

I raised a hand to interrupt him. 'I'm just saying that before I accept the job, I want to be convinced your client's innocent. But not of course at my expense.'

'All right.' The lawyer took a yellow envelope from his jacket pocket.

I counted the notes. 'Fine. Does your client realize that if I take the case, it'll cost him real money? On top of expenses, I'll have to take account of the risks involved.'

Bonotto smiled, got up and began to put on his overcoat.

'As a matter of fact, I don't come cheap either. But professional criminals like Corradi are prudent men—they have to be. I'm confident the legal fund he has set aside for just such eventualities as these will cover our fees.'

'Whose idea was it to come to me? Yours or your client's?'

'It was my idea.'

'And what did he say?'

'Just that he trusted my judgment.' Bonotto picked up his cell phone from the bar and left.

Virna came and sat at my table. 'New job?' she asked.

'Could be,' I said. 'You're tired,' I added, looking at her face.

She smiled. 'Not too tired to ask you back to my place when the club closes.'

I smiled back. 'Okay.'

'So don't overdo the drink,' she said, heading back to wait at the tables.

Virna was my girl. Her real name was Giovanna but, owing to a passing resemblance to Virna Lisi in a famous toothpaste ad, everybody called her Virna. She was forty and had the charged expression and abrupt manner of someone whose life had not been easy. I liked her a lot. She loved me. All in all, we got along fine, even if she was a little too keen to organize my life and stop me drinking.

I got to know her when she first came to work at the club as a waitress. Like everybody else, she thought the joint belonged to Rudy Scanferla, the barman, whereas in fact it was mine. Rudy had kindly agreed to manage it for the sake of our long friendship, not to mention the excellent wages I paid him. It was a few kilometers outside Padova in a small town that, like so many others, had sprung up thirty years earlier along the main road and was now basking in north-eastern Italy's economic miracle.

The club opened at eight in the evening and closed at four in the morning. Customers called it La Cuccia. It was warm, welcoming and discreet: a good place to sit, drink, chew the fat and hear good music—blues, mainly, my favorite kind of music. Not long ago, a singer, Eloisa Deriu, had turned up with a voice that could range from operatic arias to blues and jazz, and who had so much talent that somehow I never found the courage to tell her that before she came along nothing but blues had ever been heard at La Cuccia. I too had once been a singer, though not in Eloisa's league. But I had taken to heart the old saying that 'you can take the blues out of alcohol but you can't take alcohol out of the blues' and I would get up on stage with a few drinks inside me, and my voice would ring out as warm and moist as marsh mist. My group was called the Old Red Alligators and we even had a fan club. In fact it was my admirers who gave me the nickname Alligator. Those had been good times. But then I wound up in prison and by the time I got out my voice had dried up. After seven years of silence, all that was left was my nickname and a longing to listen. In prison I had become a skillful peacemaker, moving easily between the various criminal gangs. So when I got out I started working for lawyers who needed an entrée into organized crime to get their clients out of trouble.

I had two associates. Beniamino Rossini, also known as Old Rossini to distinguish him from his many brothers, was one of the few surviving members of the old-style criminal underworld. His mother, of Basque descent, had been a legendary smuggler and Rossini had started out, no more than a kid, helping her to move contraband goods over the Swiss border. Later he specialized in multi-million dollar robberies. His last big job had gone wrong, and the two of us had met up in prison, where I had had the pleasure of helping him out of a delicate situation involving a group of Neapolitan Camorristi.

Now Rossini was rich, fiftyish, and lived in a house by the sea at Punta Sabbioni, where he devoted his energies to smuggling goods from nearby Dalmatia: weapons, gold, caviar, girls, and people in trouble with the law. There was nothing that obliged him to help me with my investigations. He did it on account of our friendship and because he liked getting into trouble. He had a gut loathing for the new-style underworld, full of snitches and dope-peddlers, and often the cases that I worked on gave him the opportunity to settle old scores. He lived with Sylvie, a French-Algerian belly dancer. She was a fine-looking woman of about forty, with blue eyes, amber-colored skin, a resolute character, a husky smoker's voice and a genuine passion for motorbikes.

My other associate was Max the Memory, or Fat Max. He had recently got out of prison, thanks to a pardon from the Italian President. The clemency motion had actually been the result of an agreement negotiated with an anti-mafia judge whom I had had no hesitation in blackmailing. Max had been avoiding the police for a long time, owing to a matter that dated back to the Seventies. At that time, he had been in charge of counterinformation for a Far Left group and had run a whole network of informants who spied on everything and everybody.

Then, in the Eighties, several turncoats had accused him of passing information to groups engaged in armed struggle and he had been forced underground. Everyone just assumed he was in France, but in fact he hadn't left the city. Holed up in safe houses, rarely venturing out, he just went on gathering information. I used him as an analyst in a couple of investigations I was working on at that time, and his assistance proved absolutely decisive. To get in touch with him, you had to go through his woman, Marielita, a Uruguayan street musician. As it turned out, she died in my arms, killed by a hit man acting on orders from the local Brenta Mafia. Old Rossini had then gone in and restored a modicum of balance. After he got his pardon, Max moved into one of the two flats I'd had built above the club.

I looked up at the ceiling and pictured Max sitting at his desk, busily entering data in his computer or surfing the net. Later, as always, he would come down for a drink. Like everyone else, he had his vices. His fingers were yellow with nicotine and he had a hefty beer gut. Come to think of it, the only one of us in good shape was Old Rossini, with his trim and taut physique. That was the way it should be: it was his job to show some muscle. The only thing that rang a bit false was his old-fashioned moustache à la Xavier Cugat which, like the few remaining hairs on his head, had clearly been dyed.

I popped behind the counter, picked up a clean cell phone and left the club.

'Ciao, Marco,' Rossini replied at once.

'Are you busy?' I asked.

'I've got to pick up Sylvie from the nightclub at three.'

I looked at my watch. It was 10:30. 'How soon can you get here?'

'About an hour.'

'I'll wait for you at Max's.'

While Max the Memory had been in prison, I had stocked his flat with anonymous furniture bought from a local manufacturer during one of their periodic clearance sales. With his shrewd eye for pictures, carpets and lamps, Max had somehow managed to make the place warm and comfortable. Every time I walked in I couldn't help being reminded that the only personal touch in my flat was my record collection.

I found Max in his study. The walls were completely covered with reproductions of pictures by Edward Hopper, Max's favorite artist. As a Christmas present, I had given him a copy of 'Nighthawks' produced by an eminent forger and I was pleased to see that Max had given it pride of place on the wall opposite his best armchair. Rising from the club below, Eloisa Deriu's voice filled the whole room with 'Just to Sing'. Max's fingers rattled over the computer keyboard. Glancing at the screen, I recognized the face of a well-known Venetian banker.

'I was going to come down in half an hour or so,' Max said, without glancing up.

'Maybe we've got a case,' I said. 'Rossini's on his way over.' This time Max looked at me. 'What does maybe mean?'

'Just that for the time being we get paid to decide whether we like the look of it or not.'

Max snorted. 'Come on, give me a clue. Rape, drugs, child abuse . . . ?'

'Cocaine. But the guy accused may well be innocent.' I drew up a chair and helped myself to one of his untipped cigarettes. I pointed at the face on the screen. 'Why are you interested in him?'

'I received a tip-off. It seems that people have been going along to his bank to borrow money and he's been feeding them to the loan-sharks.'

'Nice people,' I commented. 'Have you got anything for me to drink?'

He waved at a drinks cabinet, where I found some Calvados. Max was drinking Jamaican beer. I drank and smoked in silence, observing Max as he worked at the computer.

Old Rossini arrived punctually, looking as elegant as ever. Under his camel-colored overcoat he was wearing one of his pin-striped gangster suits. He freed his wrists, setting the gold bracelets on his left wrist all a-jangle. They were his scalps, each one the souvenir of a score settled with a firearm. He was very proud of them.

He placed on the table a packet of Marlboro and the kind of gold cigarette lighter that was fashionable back in the Seventies, when Milan was run by syndicates from Marseilles.

'What kind of mess are you getting us into this time?' he asked, with an inquisitive smile.

'Does the name Nazzareno Corradi mean anything to you?' I asked.

'I've heard of him all right. As far as I'm aware, he's on the level.'

'He was arrested in a hotel in Jesolo on the twenty-sixth of December. He claims he went there to fetch his Colombian girlfriend who had been taken sick. But when he got to the room, instead of his girlfriend, a Colombian drug courier with eight-hundred grams of coke in his belly opened the door. And surrounding him, the drug squads from both the regular police and the Finanza.'

Old Rossini poured himself a drink. 'The twenty-sixth of December? At least he managed to miss the millennium party nightmare . . .'

I signaled to Rossini to shut up, and then recounted my conversation with Bonotto and our agreement.

'You did the right thing,' Rossini said. 'The way I see it, there are far too many Colombian coincidences. In any case, it's best to check things out. People change and Corradi may have degenerated.'

Max scratched at the stubbly beard under his chin. 'Yeah, I agree. But the lawyer has a point. For such a minor arrest, it was one hell of a police operation. They even went to the trouble of taking the mule along with them to the hotel, just to make the trap seem more convincing. And the timing is all wrong. Arías Cuevas was arrested at five in the afternoon but Corradi didn't knock on his door till three in the morning. What I'd like to know is what happened in those ten hours. Maybe Corradi was put in the frame because somebody figured his links with Colombia would help make the accusation stick.'

I got up and stretched my legs. 'You're right. The whole thing reeks of special operations. But that's still outweighed by Corradi's known links with Colombia and the easy money to be made from coke trafficking.'

'What are you thinking of doing?' Old Rossini asked.

'I thought I'd have a word with Corradi's Colombian girl-friend and then the hotel staff. But the main thing is to set up a direct line to Corradi. I want to hear the story the way he tells it, without Bonotto's spin.'

Max uncapped another beer. 'A direct line? What do you mean? A cell phone or a bent cop?'

'A cop.'

Rossini snapped his fingers. 'I know a corporal in the prison police who's just the man.'

Nazzareno Corradi lived on the edge of Ormelle, a small village not far from Treviso. The house, awkward-looking and pretentious in its architecture and color-scheme, seemed just like what it was—the home of a nouveau-riche gangster. It was strategically isolated, ringed by a thick boxwood hedge, and guarded by a pair of rottweilers. Rossini and I looked it over for a moment or two. Then we got out of the car. Max had stayed at home. He wasn't one for wearing out shoe leather.

Corradi's girlfriend opened the door. Victoria Rodriguez Gomez was a beautiful, dark-haired young woman, who must have been in her early twenties. She had a perfectly formed oval face, full lips, skin with a dash of Colombian coffee to it, and a whole lot of curves. Corradi could be forgiven for losing his head over her.

Old Rossini took hold of her hand and grazed it lightly with his lips. I tried to be more professional, confining myself to a simple greeting. 'We're working for Nazzareno's lawyer,' I explained. 'We'd like to have a word with you about what's happened.'

'I was expecting you.' Victoria beckoned us to follow her and led us into an expensively and sumptuously furnished lounge. There were silver-framed photos of the joyous couple all over the place. 'I'd like to thank you for what you are doing for my man,' she said, with a display of emotion.

'He pays us, end of story,' Rossini said icily. It was time to stop drooling over her beauty.

'Does Nazzareno peddle coke?' I asked.

'No, he doesn't.'

'What about you?' Rossini insisted.

'No way.'

'You're Colombian, right? From Bogotá. The mule is Colombian. From Bogotá. And Nazzareno has been on several trips to Colombia. To Bogotá.'

Victoria picked up one of several framed photos from a small table and clasped it to her breast. It portrayed Corradi and Victoria standing on either side of a man who was embracing them affectionately. 'Nazzareno came back home with me one time to meet my family,' Victoria stated calmly and firmly, in almost flawless Italian. 'Look. I know that before you agree to take the case you want to be absolutely certain Nazzareno isn't a trafficker, and that's as it should be. But if you're asking me why he of all people was lured into a trap, I just don't know.'

I was thirsty. I looked around, but all I could see on the drinks table were bottles of amaretto and grappa. I was going to have to wait a while before any Calvados came my way.

'This story about a trap . . . you know what doesn't add up?' I asked, looking squarely at Victoria. 'The fact that everything hung on Nazzareno not reaching you on your cell phone. He claims he received a call informing him you had been taken ill in a hotel room in Jesolo. And he also claims he tried to ring you, but you were unobtainable because you'd gone to meet your girlfriends in a lap-dance joint where there was no signal. But the cops couldn't have known that, and leaving things to chance is not the way they work. Do you see what I'm getting at? Nazzareno's story just doesn't stand up.'

Victoria looked me straight in the eye. 'But it's the truth . . . I often go there. Everyone knows that. Maybe the cops had us under surveillance.'

Rossini and I exchanged glances. The interview was over.

'Excuse our blunt manners,' I said, getting up, 'but this case is a tangled mess, your man is in big trouble, and we have to be sure we're working for the right client.'

Victoria walked us to the door. She was still clasping the photo of Corradi. 'Nazzareno took me out of the lap-dance joint,' she began. 'Before I met him, I used to work all night and sleep during the day. I was terrified that that was how I'd end my life. I owe him everything. There is no way I would ever have introduced him to the narcos.' She closed the door.

'She didn't say she loved him though,' I remarked.

'You're expecting too much,' Old Rossini said. 'Let's face it, they've both gained a lot from the relationship. Corradi would never have got to screw a bombshell like that free of charge.'

'Do you reckon she's telling the truth?'

'It's too soon to say. What about you?'

'She seems sincere all right. All the same, this evening I think I'll go and have a chat with her old colleagues at the lap-dance joint in Eraclea.'

We had lunch at a restaurant in Jesolo, not far from the Pensione Zodiaco. This was Rossini's home turf and we were treated like VIPs. I made do with a few forkfuls of risotto alla pescatora, but Rossini got stuck into a whole variety of different antipasti. When we had finished eating, we invited the restaurateur over to our table for a coffee.

'What do you know about the Zodiaco?' Rossini asked.

'It's busiest in the summer, mainly. It's family run. They give you bed, breakfast and an evening meal and it's cheap. All in all, a quiet little hotel.'

'Drugs, girls . . . ?'

'No. None of that stuff.'

'But ten days ago they arrested a Colombian there with eight-hundred grams of coke.'

'Yeah, I heard about that. Whoever told him to go to the Zodiaco knew it was the place to use if you don't want to attract attention. In the winter, there's nothing but passing trade.'

At the hotel reception desk, we found a man sprawled across a 1960s leather armchair that was stylistically in perfect harmony with the rest of the room's furnishings. He must have been over sixty. Short and skinny, he wore a light brown suit, white shirt and a red tie fastened in a slender knot. It was early afternoon and he was glued to the television.

Old Rossini pointed at the TV set. 'Anna Identici. She was

one of my all-time favorites. She used to sing at Communist Party festivals. "Era Bello Il Mio Ragazzo" always brought tears to my eyes.'

'Yeah, I remember it well.'

'Afternoon. You want a room?' the man asked, without peeling his eyes from the screen.

I pulled out my cigarettes, offered Rossini one and looked around. The place looked clean and decent enough. Your classic small hotel with the same summer customers year-in year-out for thirty years, and every day identical. Mornings at the seaside, followed by lunch and a quiet nap. Then back to the beach. Dinner at seven on the dot: pasta, cheese and salad. A game of canasta and then at eleven, bed.

Our silence forced the man to pay us some attention. 'I did ask if you wanted a room.'

'No, thank you,' I replied politely. 'We'd like to know what happened here during the night of the twenty-sixth of December. All the details.'

'Who are you?' asked the man warily, settling his metal-framed spectacles on his nose.

Rossini broke in drily. 'What's your preference? Reporters, lawyers, priests, ratcatchers? We can be whoever you want us to be.'

'I don't get it.'

'Are you the owner of this hotel?' I asked pleasantly.

'Yes, I am.'

'Good. That means we're talking to the right person. We just want to know what happened on that particular night, when the police arrived here with the Colombian, and then later on when they arrested the man who came knocking on the Colombian's door,' I explained, in a conciliatory tone.

The hotelier shook his head vigorously. 'I can't tell you. So please leave now. Otherwise I'll call the police.'

I looked at the hotel price list on the wall behind his head.

Then I pulled out my wallet and placed on the counter the price of a double room for a week. 'You must forgive me for insisting, but it's important. Besides, nobody will know,' I said.

I could tell that although he was sorely tempted by the offer he still couldn't quite make up his mind. Rossini decided to tip the balance.

'Hurry up, grab the cash and start talking. Because if you don't, I'll break one of your arms now and then come back next week and break the other.'

Rossini had issued this threat in a flat tone quite free of malice, and the man was now ready to talk. I guess he just needed a good reason to accept the bribe.

The hotelier pocketed the money and spoke for five minutes straight. He wasn't a great storyteller, a bit weak on detail and confused in places, but we managed to piece together a clear enough picture of what had happened. The room had been booked over the phone a few days before Christmas by a man with a strong local accent. He had said that a Spanish guest of his would be arriving at about 6:30 P.M. on the twenty-sixth and that he would only be staying one night. He had said he would drop round the same evening in person to pay the bill.

At 7 P.M. on the twenty-sixth, the Spaniard still hadn't shown up. At five past seven, the man had phoned to find out whether his guest had arrived, and from then on he phoned every half-hour. Just before nine, a captain from the Guardia di Finanza and an officer from Venice police headquarters had turned up at reception, both in plain clothes, and discreetly showed the hotelier their service ID.

The cops had enquired about the room booked for the Spaniard and asked for information on the other people staying at the hotel. When the man who had booked the room phoned back to hear whether his guest had arrived, the hotelier, acting on orders from the two cops, told him that the

Spaniard had already checked into the room, but had just popped out to get some cigarettes. The man on the phone then announced that he was coming over to the hotel and would be there in about twenty minutes. At this point, the cops had asked the hotelier to disappear for a while, saying that they would look after reception personally, and if there were any problems with the other hotel customers they would call him.

The hotelier had then withdrawn, with his wife, into their private apartment. Less than half an hour later, the cops had knocked on his door to say everything was fine and would he mind coming along to the Commissariat the following afternoon to sign a statement. They had then thanked him for his cooperation and left.

At midnight, before he had locked the door and retired for the night—the hotelier preferred to give his clients the key to the door rather than pay a night porter's wages—the cops had returned. They had brought with them a guy who must have been some kind of a foreigner: he had a moustache, his hair was slicked down with brilliantine, and he had handcuffs on his wrists. The police had asked the hotelier to keep out of the way till the following morning, saying the hotel was needed for a major police operation.

He had obeyed without a word. He was particularly frightened of the captain from the Finanza and didn't wish to do anything whatsoever to upset him. He had fallen badly behind with his accounts and didn't want anyone poking their noses in. He hadn't the faintest idea what had happened during that night but at a certain point—around three in the morning—he had heard someone yelling. Some of the people staying at the hotel had heard it too. The following morning he'd had to make up a story about a guest having a row with his girlfriend.

The next day, when he arrived at the Commissariat to make his statement, something odd had happened. In the prepared account of events they read out to him, there was no mention of the first time they had asked him to 'disappear' for thirty minutes or so, between nine and ten o'clock the previous evening.

'But you took care not to bring up this oversight, am I right?'

The hotelier removed his specs and began to clean them with a handkerchief exactly the same shade of brown as his suit. 'It was none of my business. They told me I'd be called upon to testify at the trial but that I'd only need to confirm what I'd already told the police.' He sat back down in his armchair in front of the TV. Anna Identici had been replaced at the microphone by Nilla Pizzi, warbling the usual tear-jerker.

'What do you think?' I asked my associate, when we got out of the hotel.

Rossini fiddled with his bracelets. 'I don't know. That guy's account wasn't all that clear . . . Maybe the first trap drew a blank. But then the cops would hardly have left the Zodiaco. Above all, they wouldn't have told the hotelier everything was just fine and that he should come along to the Commissariat the following day.'

'No. Something must have happened that both the police and the Finanza are keen to cover up. The holes in the statement they got the hotelier to sign are clear enough evidence of that.'

'Maybe Corradi knows something. It's time we had a chat with him.'

Vincenzo Mansutti, a corporal in Venice's prison police service, was a man of strict habit: every evening, on leaving the Santa Maria Maggiore prison, he stopped off at a nearby osteria for a quick drink. He was forty, his career was going nowhere, and he was obsessed with Oriental nightclub hostesses whose company, on the lousy salary he earned, he could ill afford to keep. Until, that is, he had run into Rossini at a nightclub.

Mansutti had been slavering over a barely passable Filipino

girl who was doing very little business that evening. He kept making eyes at her and every now and then flashed her a grin. The girl seemed irritated with this Italian who instead of stepping forward and buying himself some time in her company had just sat there and ogled.

Old Rossini had been observing the scene and had noted the distinctive fragrance of cop that Mansutti gave off. The waiter confirmed Rossini's suspicions, informing him that what he was looking at was in fact a prison cop. Rossini realized at once that he had been presented with a golden opportunity. He had another word with the waiter and then a couple of minutes later looked on as the Filipino hostess walked up to Mansutti, took him by the hand and led him over to a booth where a bottle of champagne was waiting for them.

Rossini let an hour slip by before going over and introducing himself. 'Hi. I'm Beniamino Rossini. This is all on me and, if you feel like prolonging the evening's entertainment, this young lady will be happy to spend a couple of hours with you in one of the backrooms.'

'How come you're so friendly?' Mansutti had asked, frowning suspiciously.

'Because you're a prison cop and I'm the kind of person who's liable to end up one day as a guest of yours. I'd like to know I've got a friend . . .'

Mansutti had been quick-witted enough to counter, 'What, for a single fuck?'

'If this joint and its personnel are to your liking, I can open an account for you. You can come and go as you like, have a good time and pay nothing. But the day I snap my fingers, I want first-rate service.'

'You've got a deal,' Mansutti had replied, with a sly little grin that didn't escape Rossini's notice.

'One last thing: find out who I am. That way you won't try to rip me off.'

'Okay, okay. I have no intention of ripping anyone off.'

'Then congratulations. You've just become a bent cop.'

So when Mansutti saw us walk into the osteria, he knew right away it was payback time. In a single gulp he emptied the glass of verduzzo the barman had just poured him. Then he placed a couple of banknotes on the counter, left the bar, and ducked into a narrow street.

He stopped almost immediately and waited for us, looking tense. Maybe he had hoped this moment would never come. Rossini looked him straight in the eye and gave him a friendly smile. 'There's a really cute chick who's just arrived from Thailand. She works at a nightclub near Pordenone but I can arrange for you to meet her.'

Mansutti took a deep breath. 'Somehow I don't think you've come here just to tell me that.'

Rossini's expression hardened. 'You're right. I've come to ask you a little favor.' He extracted a cell phone from his pocket and handed it to Mansutti. 'We need to talk to Nazzareno Corradi, Block C, cell twenty-one.'

Mansutti turned white. 'I can't do it. They'll find it the first time they do a search.'

Rossini shook his head. 'No, they won't. Because you'll have it. You hand it to him just before we call and as soon as we're done you take it back off him.'

'There's no way I can take it into his cell. He's not on his own. Besides, he's under special surveillance. Police head-quarters have made the governor put an informant in with him.'

Rossini and I exchanged glances. Mansutti was turning out to be a mine of information.

'What's his name? What's the snitch's name?' Rossini demanded.

'Angiò. Rossano Angiò.'

'What's he in for?'

'Dealing ecstasy.'

'A hero of our times,' I remarked. Then I turned to Mansutti. 'You're a corporal, right? I'm sure you don't do guard duties on the block. Where can you approach Corradi without attracting attention?'

'In the exercise yard, I guess. There are some toilets near the control post. I could leave the phone there while I'm doing my routine check before the prisoners come down, and then pick it up again at the end of the hour.'

'When is Block C's turn in the yard?' I asked.

'From two to three in the afternoon.'

'We'll call at ten past two on the dot. How are you going to put Corradi in the picture?'

'That won't be a problem. Tomorrow I'll make sure I relieve the other corporal at the control post. More to the point, how many times will you be wanting to call?'

'As many as it takes,' replied Rossini. 'Keep the phone in your pocket at all times, with the battery well charged. We'll let you know the evening before we make a call.'

Mansutti took a few steps then turned around. 'What about the chick from Thailand? What's the deal?'

Rossini took a folded piece of paper from his inside coat pocket. 'Call this number. They'll tell you where and when. It's all set up.'

'You've got him on a nice tight leash,' I said, as we watched Mansutti walking away.

Rossini chuckled and shook his head. 'The Filipino girl told me he spends the whole time nuzzling and sniffing at her. He's a total head-case, but he'll do as he's told. He's got too much to lose to jerk us around.'

A little before midnight we arrived at the Black Baron in Eraclea to check out Victoria's story.

It was one of the area's most fashionable nightspots, with

subdued lighting, fifth-rate music and family men out to get their kicks. On the main floor, the girls danced topless while a bunch of half-drunk slobs slipped banknotes under the elastic of their panties.

After a quick chat with the landlord, I followed Old Rossini over to one of the booths reserved for the more intimate kinds of display performed for a limited number of customers. We had just sat down when a blonde girl walked in. She had a hard, heavily made-up face and a somewhat ungainly body, but she had big tits, the essential prerequisite for anyone in that line of work. She said she was Romanian, her name was Vera, and she had been in Italy a year.

She gave us a huge grin. 'I can either dance or . . .' and here she made an unambiguous gesture with her mouth. 'No problem,' she went on. 'You just give me a little extra present.'

'If they find out you're offering your clients that type of service on the side, you're going to get badly roughed up,' Rossini warned. 'It's enough to get the whole joint closed down.'

The girl sat down between us and poured herself a glass from a bottle of Moët & Chandon. The label was a fairly skillful fake and the bottle in fact contained the cheapest variety of fizzy wine. One of many standard nightclub scams.

'Oh, they don't mind if I do stuff with clients. The clients certainly don't call me into a booth so they can watch me dance. I'm not beautiful. I have to do what I can.'

'Whereas Victoria was really in demand, right?' I asked.

'Oh, yes. But she is beautiful, really a beautiful woman.'

'Does she come and see you much?'

'Sure, at least once a week.'

'Including the night of the twenty-sixth of December?'

Vera glared at us. 'Hey, that was the evening they arrested her man. You're not the police, are you?'

I reassured her. 'No, of course we're not. Well?'

'Yes, she was here with us. She spent some time in the bar

and then went to the dressing-room for a chat with the girls who were resting.'

'How did she seem? Relaxed?'

'Sure. We talked about the shitty owners of lap-dance joints and had a good laugh. We were laughing the whole time.'

'When did she leave?'

'Some time after four.'

I pulled out my wallet and handed her a good tip. Vera gave us a little goodbye wave and went off to chase other clients. Rossini called the waiter over. 'Take this crap away and bring me a vodka, the good stuff, and iced.'

'I'll have a Calvados.'

'What Vera says backs up Victoria's story,' Rossini remarked, checking the signal on his cell phone. 'Huh! Down here in this hole, cell phones are useless, and she was here till the place closed.'

'Right.'

'If we decide to take the job and help Corradi, how are you thinking of proceeding?'

'Well, it's not going to be the most straightforward of cases. This time we're going to have to deal directly with cops and magistrates. They're the only ones really in the picture. And they're not going to give anything away if they can help it.'

'Maybe there's a way we can load the dice.'

'If they let us . . .'

I got back to La Cuccia just in time to see Virna. She was warming up the engine of her car. It was a bitterly cold night, everything covered with a white shroud of frost, and Virna's nose was icy. When I told her I wouldn't be coming to sleep at her place that night because I wanted to be alone, she stuck it right up against my neck in retaliation.

I stretched out on the couch in the lounge and aimed the remote at the stereo. There was a silence, then the voice of

Robben Ford pitched into 'Prison of Love'. I reached out a hand and picked up a bottle of Calvados. I removed the cap and sniffed at the contents. It put me in a good mood straight away. I ought to have focused on the case but I just couldn't. I let myself go, to the rhythm of the blues. It was going to be a good night.

L a Tía hugged her coat close as she hurried down the steps onto the runway. Never in her life had she felt such intense cold. Aisa followed just behind, lunging and tottering in the high-heeled boots she had persuaded La Tía to buy for her at the duty-free shop in Amsterdam. In the airport bus, La Tía took a sip of Blanco, before handing the bottle to Aisa, who barely moistened her lips with it. She loathed that low-grade rum with its taste of aniseed, but Doña Rosa was the kind of woman you didn't like to disobey.

Wrapped up in somewhat démodé winter suits and coats, they looked just like any other South American middleclass mother and daughter, over in Europe for the holidays. Although their Colombian passports appeared to be in order, Customs picked through their baggage with extreme thoroughness. In the end La Tía and Aisa got the entrance stamp they needed on their tourist visas and were let through.

Doña Rosa, in any case, didn't intend to stay long, just the time it took to sort out a couple of business matters. She gave the taxi-driver the name of a hotel in Jesolo where Colombian girls employed as nightclub hostesses in the Venice area generally stayed. She had booked three double rooms. Alacrán and another killer, Luis Fernando Jaramillo, along with two women gang members, would be joining them that afternoon. They had arrived at Lourdes a couple of days earlier, and would cross the Italian border with a coachload of the faithful. La Tía had ordered them to bring her a statue of the

Virgin full of holy water. Our Lady of Lourdes. Our Lady of the narcos.

A couple of hours before our telephone appointment with Nazzareno Corradi, Rossini, Max and I met in Max's study. I stuck a handful of salt peanuts in my mouth and drowned them with a gulp of Calvados. I had only just woken up and hadn't had time for breakfast.

'Let's see if we can't keep out of the cops' way,' Old Rossini advised. 'That business at the hotel stinks of trouble.'

'I couldn't agree more,' said Max. 'It would be better to come at it from a totally different angle.'

'Loading the dice in our favor?' Rossini asked.

'Precisely. We exploit the fact that Corradi and Arías Cuevas are in the same prison and see to it that the mule submits a voluntary statement to the investigating magistrate to the effect that he's never met Corradi in his life, and that the police forced him into putting on that charade at the hotel.'

I got up from the armchair and fetched my cigarettes. 'But it may not work. We would have to keep Corradi's lawyer in the dark, get whatever lawyer the court has assigned to the Colombian to agree to see things our way, and then come up with an offer that the mule finds attractive. The problem is that by now the cops will already have promised him a maximum two-year sentence, so I don't really see him wanting to change his story.'

Rossini shook his head. 'But look at it this way. He's in a prison on the other side of the world, he's on his own, and he's not got a penny to his name. I don't think he'll be too hard to work on.'

Max looked up from his notes. 'First, Arías Cuevas gave the police a description of his Italian contact that was nothing like Corradi. Then, at the hotel, when the mule opened his door and came face to face with Corradi, he started yelling "Get out of here, get out of here" in Spanish, giving everyone the impression he knew Corradi. This will all be in the records and it's not a bad place to start if we want to muddy the waters while we look for a way out.'

'Max is right,' Rossini chipped in. 'If we take this job and Corradi agrees to go behind his lawyer's back, there's a good chance we can fuck over both the cops and the magistrate.'

I stuck a few more peanuts in my mouth. 'They don't seem all that keen to be fucked over.'

Corporal Mansutti had been as good as his word. Corradi replied as soon as the cell phone vibrated.

'I'm known as Alligator. Your lawyer reckons I can help you out.'

'I know who you are and I want to thank you for what you're doing,' Corradi said, in a rasping voice that carried with it a hint of cigarettes and sleepless nights.

'You're in deep shit.'

'I've got absolutely fuck-all to do with any of this.'

'There are too many Colombian coincidences,' I replied. 'Besides, why should they pick you?'

'You're looking at it from the wrong angle. It's precisely because of my Colombian connections that they chose me for the frame. And what's their motive? That jeweler's store robbery years back. Nunziante, the flatfoot in charge of the investigations, always swore he'd get back at me.'

'Forgive me for asking this, but I have to know . . . Was Nunziante just going on what he'd heard or . . .'

'No, he wasn't. It was me all right. I killed the two patrolmen. Then when it came to trial I got acquitted because they didn't have a scrap of evidence. But somebody who knew exactly what had happened—maybe even one of the boys who had taken part in the robbery—went and blabbed to Nunziante. So when they took me to the Commissariat in

Jesolo the other day, Nunziante gave me a smack in the jaw and told me he'd known all along that I'd done the patrolmen, and to prove it he mentioned a particular detail that never came out during the investigation.'

'What a mess. They'll stop at nothing to make you pay.'

'I know the rules. If they'd pulled me in for something I'd actually done, I'd have gone quietly, just tried a little damage limitation. But when it comes to cocaine—I've got absolutely nothing to do with it, never have. And I could be looking at twenty years.'

'Do you think you can get to the Colombian without drawing attention to yourself?'

'He's on another block, but with a bit of luck I can probably manage it.'

'Okay. Set up a meeting. If the mule's prepared to make a statement putting you in the clear, we'll deal with his lawyer.'

'Nunziante is not going to let it go that easy.'

'That's true. But a statement from the Colombian could undermine the prosecution case to the point where they couldn't block a request for house arrest.'

'Right. Then I'd take myself off on an extended vacation.'

'Yeah, something like that. I'll call you the same time tomorrow so you can tell me what agreement you've reached with the Colombian. Just one more thing. Your cellmate, Rossano Angiò, is a police plant.'

'I thought as much. Far too buddy-buddy.'

'Corradi . . .'

'Yeah?'

'Don't tell anyone about this direct line. Not even your woman. It could get dangerous for everyone involved.'

'Don't worry. Victoria is right outside the loop and it's best she stays that way.'

I put the phone down and glanced at my two associates. Rossini offered me a cigarette. 'Corradi knows what he's doing.

He'll find a way to talk the Colombian into testifying for the defense,' he remarked, before saying goodbye. He had to go and take delivery of a load of caviar from Dalmatia. Besides which, there was nothing much for us to do till we recontacted Corradi the next day.

I called Renato Bonotto and told him we had decided to accept the case. Corradi had seemed to us to be on the level. Naturally I omitted to tell Bonotto anything precise about our plan. It would have placed him in an impossible position, professionally speaking, and it would have permanently undermined the trust between us. Anyway, he was really glad to hear the news and made me promise to keep him updated.

'What do we know about the Colombian's lawyer?' I then asked Max.

Max thumbed through his notes. 'Francesco Beltrame, attached to Venice City Court, thirty-one years old, appointed by the magistrate to represent Arías Cuevas under the provisions of the free legal assistance scheme. A smart kid waiting for his big break.'

'Like thousands of others,' I remarked.

'Right. Have you still got that old contact of yours in Paris?'

I stared at Max in puzzlement. 'Sure. But what's that got to do with anything?'

'You could call him and see if he knows any Colombian exiles who can give us some information about our trafficker. It's just possible we might find out something we can use in our negotiations.'

'Excellent idea. I'll try straight away.'

Alessio Sperlinga, nicknamed Ciliegia on account of the spherical cherry-red growth in the middle of his right cheek, was a chubby, friendly sort of guy. Originally he was from Como, near the Swiss border, but I got to know him in prison. He had ended up there, as so often happened, owing to a turncoat who up until that moment had been his best friend.

Luckily the accusation that he was a member of an armed gang hadn't kept him in prison too long. But when he got out, he had preferred to emigrate to France rather than start again from scratch in his home town. He hadn't lost his passion for far left politics and spent years gathering material for a book on our generation of political militants and misfits—but he never got round to writing it. He worked for an IT company and, from what I had heard, had become a first-class chess player.

'Ciao, Ciliegia!'

'Alligator, how are things with you?'

'Not bad. I need a favor.'

'You wouldn't have phoned otherwise.'

'Are you in contact with any Colombians?'

'FARC or ELN?' he asked, naming the country's two main guerrilla organizations.

'I've no idea. I'm looking into the case of a cocaine trafficker snatched at Venice airport. I need some background.'

'I can always ask around. I'll give you an email address where you can send me the trafficker's details and, the most important thing, his photo. The Colombians are past masters at inventing fake identities for themselves.'

'The photo that appeared in *Nuova Venezia* is pretty good quality,' I reassured him.

We chatted for a while. Finally, I asked him if he ever felt homesick for Italy. 'Not in the slightest, Alligator. It's not that I'm up to all that much here, but back in Italy I really wouldn't have a clue what to do with myself. I'd feel even more cut-off from everything going on around me.'

I said goodbye and glanced at Max. He had been listening in to the conversation on the speakerphone. 'Your friend's right,' he said. 'The left has been marginalized for good. It's not our world any longer. For a brief moment, we held it in the palm of our hand. Then they snatched it away again.'

I shrugged. 'I never had your dreams of revolution, Max, so I haven't lost anything. All I ever wanted was to be a blues singer. Right now I'm happy to be where I am. Going off somewhere else no longer makes the slightest sense.'

I returned to my apartment and dozed off on the couch listening to Joe Louis Walker singing 'My Dignity'. By the time I went downstairs to the club it was late evening. Maurizio Camardi, a friend of mine who played the saxophone, had organized a session with Eloisa, our resident singer. It was a really enjoyable night. At four, I took Virna home and we went to bed. I lit a cigarette. She rested her head on my chest and I started to stroke her hair.

'We've been together for a year and a half now, but you've never told me anything about yourself.' This came straight out of the blue. Her voice was very calm, almost sad.

'What do you mean?'

'That you never let me in on what you're thinking. It's just . . . I've realized I don't really know you.'

'In my line of work, there's no room for sharing secrets.'

'It's got nothing to do with your work. You just never let on what you really think or feel. You're nice and kind to me, you make me laugh, we have a good time together, but somehow you shut me out of your life.'

I took a long drag on my cigarette, recalling my conversation with Max a few hours earlier. Virna was right of course. But how could I ever explain to her that the most intimate part of my existence was over, buried under a mountain of rubble? Or that the only thing I had left to share with anyone was this messy day-to-day life I led?

'There's nothing I can do about it, Virna. It's just the way it is.'

'That's not true. Things can change. That's why people get together.'

I didn't reply and she fell asleep, snoring softly. I turned to look at her. Tiredness was mercilessly deepening the lines she had acquired working nights and falling in love with men who, like me, had never been able to offer her anything. I smiled at her, and lightly kissed the corner of her mouth.

Nazzareno Corradi was euphoric. 'The meeting with the Colombian went like a dream. He'll do anything to avoid being sent back to Colombia. He's demanding cast-iron guarantees from a lawyer, money up-front, and several minor internal prison favors.'

'Well, it won't be easy to get around the deportation order once he's completed his sentence,' I objected.

'Make something up, Alligator,' Corradi barked. 'This guy's far more scared of going home than of staying in jail.'

'What did you make of him?'

'He's a nobody.'

'From now on, avoid any contact with him. We'll go and have a word with his lawyer later today.'

Francesco Beltrame had been born into a family of lawyers. The stately palace near the Rialto, not far from the Venice City Courts, had on its door a plate bearing the name of not one but three lawyers called Beltrame.

The secretary brought it to our attention that we didn't have an appointment. 'Legal problems are like that,' Max said thoughtfully, 'they come up all of a sudden and are often urgent.' After about forty minutes, she showed us into the young lawyer's office.

Tall, slim, with a modish goatee and wearing a midnight-blue tailored suit, Beltrame greeted us with a handshake and invited us to sit down in small armchairs opposite his desk.

We were one chair short and Beltrame went to fetch it himself from the ante-room. I glanced around to get some idea of the character we were dealing with. The decor was up- to-the-minute and pricey, the work of a well-known Venetian designer, clearly a present from Beltrame's daddy. Still, there was no doubting that Junior too had a taste for money.

He turned a smile on us that he must have practiced a thousand times in front of the mirror. 'What can I do for you? Messrs . . .'

Max scratched the stubble on his neck. 'Our names don't matter that much. Let's just say we've come here to do a friend a favor.'

Beltrame, unruffled, nodded at Max to continue. I liked the kid. He was wide awake.

'You've been appointed by the court to provide free representation to Guillermo Arías Cuevas, a Colombian national, presently detained at Santa Maria Maggiore on international drugs trafficking charges. We have no doubts whatsoever as to your professional abilities and are quite confident that Arías Cuevas will receive the best possible defense, but we are also conscious of the derisory nature of the fees disbursed to court-appointed lawyers. We have therefore decided generously to supplement the aforesaid fees in order to ensure that your professional services are remunerated at their just worth.'

Beltrame looked us over slyly. 'Very kind of you I'm sure. I suppose you gentlemen are in no way connected with the activities of Arías Cuevas . . .'

'You're on the wrong track,' Rossini snapped. 'We are not looking for anything from the Colombian. We just want you to represent him properly.'

'Exactly,' said Max, in his habitual calm and friendly tone of voice. 'We would like Arías Cuevas to be represented with special care, and feel that that care should be appropriately remunerated.'

'But you don't want him to appoint me directly as his defense lawyer. Formally speaking, Arías Cuevas must remain a legal-assistance case, right?'

Instead of replying, I extracted a yellow envelope from my jacket pocket and deposited it on the table. 'Ten million lire. Tax-free.'

Beltrame stared at the envelope for a long time. 'What am I risking?' he asked apprehensively.

'Nothing at all,' Max hurried to reassure him. 'All you've got to do is stick to procedures.'

Beltrame wasn't yet convinced. 'The Colombian is collaborating with the police. He's struck a deal with them . . .'

Max smiled benevolently. 'Why don't you go and see him. I'm certain you'll give him the best possible advice.'

Beltrame reached out and took the envelope. 'As it happens, I don't have to be in court tomorrow morning. I guess I can find the time to interview a client at the prison.'

On the way back to La Cuccia, on an autostrada plunged in freezing milky-white fog, we drove along to the sound of Taj Mahal singing 'Lovin' in My Baby's Eyes'. After a while I leaned forward and removed the cassette. 'Virna is beginning to show signs of weariness,' I said to my friends, and told them of the conversation that Virna and I had had the previous night.

From his seat behind me, Max clapped me on my right shoulder to express his solidarity. 'I know what you're feeling, Marco. But try not to lose her. Virna is special.'

Old Rossini was drumming his fingers on the steering wheel. 'Honestly, guys, I don't understand you,' he burst out.

'In fact, I've never understood you. That goes not just for the two of you but for everyone else I've ever met, whether in prison or on the outside, who was ever part of your precious "generation". What really happened? What does it amount to? They gave you a little slap on your little behinds and all of a sudden something died inside you. Please! I spent a total of fifteen years in prison. As a child I suffered hunger. My family was persecuted by the Nazis because my mother was a Jew who smuggled contraband. My first and last wife cheated on me with my lawyer. And here I am, fresh as a daisy and twice as pretty, having the time of my life.'

'It's not the same thing,' I objected.

'Of course it is,' Rossini hit back angrily. 'Virna is right, snap out of it. Wake up, deal with your past once and for all. Get over it.'

I turned around to Max, hoping for some support, but he was gazing out into the fog. I pushed the cassette back in.

'You're unbearable, Beniamino, when you do your wise old gangster routine.'

The head of security at a large department store in Mestre received a call from a floorwalker assigned to the third floor.

'Russo? This is Scavazzon. There are two foreign couples, possibly South Americans, stealing underwear off the shelves.'

'I'll be right there.'

Russo had worked for the police for years and had acquired a sharp eye for certain kinds of situations. He spotted the four thieves immediately. Their technique was tried and tested, but as old as the hills. The two women used their supposed inability to understand any Italian to monopolize the attention of the shop assistants, while the two men discreetly stuffed underwear into a small travelling bag.

Russo took his cell phone from his belt and called the Carabinieri, explaining that the two men looked as if they might cause trouble if arrested inside the store. The Carabinieri intercepted all four shoplifters as they were leaving. A small crowd of onlookers formed as the thieves were bundled into the police van. The last to get in was Aurelio Uribe Barragán, better known as Alacrán.

The thieves were driven straight to the provincial headquarters of the Carabinieri, where they were taken to separate interview rooms, identified and questioned. They were then transferred to prison to await trial, the women to Giudecca, the men to Santa Maria Maggiore.

'What are these two in for?' the duty sergeant asked as Alacrán and Jaramillo were led into the admissions office.

'Attempted theft of socks and panties,' replied a young Carabiniere as he removed their handcuffs.

'They're for trial and deportation,' commented the officer wearily. 'They'll be here two days at most.'

The new prisoners were again identified, painstakingly searched and their photographs taken. Jaramillo was a good talker and his face was less menacing than Alacrán's. As he took off his trousers, he asked the duty sergeant, half in Italian, half in Spanish, whether there were any other Colombians in the prison.

'Just one,' the officer replied. 'A drug trafficker arrested at the airport.'

Jaramillo asked him if there was any chance they could be put in the same cell as their compatriot, to keep each other company.

The sergeant looked at Jaramillo. He shouldn't really have allowed it, given that the Colombian trafficker was a police collaborator and as such required protection. But these two guys were just petty thieves and the cells were already so overcrowded that the other prisoners were sure to protest if forced to make room for new arrivals. In the end, it was this that persuaded the duty sergeant to let the Colombians have their way.

'All right,' he said. Then he turned to a young prison guard and gave the order: 'Accompany these two to Cell 23, Block D.'

Guillermo Arías Cuevas was stretched out on his bed, enjoying a quiet smoke. Corradi had supplied him with cigarettes, cooking equipment and utensils so he would no longer be forced to eat prison food. Another couple of days and he would even have new clothes and shoes. At last he would be able to turn up for the exercise hour in the yard dressed like a man, free of the shabby, crumpled suit he had been wearing day-in day-out ever since he was arrested.

Arías Cuevas was also feeling very pleased with his lawyer,

who had come to see him that morning. Beltrame had listened with interest when Guillermo told him that he intended to make a voluntary statement to the magistrate clearing his Italian co-defendant of any involvement in the crime. His lawyer had advised him on which details to leave out and which to put in, and had promised to go straight to the magistrate with a request that Guillermo be re-interviewed. The lawyer had even given Guillermo his earnest assurance that he would not be deported to Colombia—and, for Guillermo, that was a matter of life and death.

As he heard the key turning in his cell door, Guillermo was just thinking that living in Italy might turn out to be quite all right. After a while, he would get back in touch with Ruben and set up a new coke smuggling operation: Ruben would send the mules over while he, Guillermo, would take charge of distribution and sales.

When the door opened, Arías Cuevas looked up, wondering who it might be. Two men entered his cell, their faces hidden by the piles of blankets, pillows and sheets they were carrying in their arms. The guard closed the door at once, failing to notice the expression of terror that contorted Arías Cuevas' face the moment he saw, standing before him, Alacrán and Jaramillo.

'Take it easy, hombre, easy,' whispered Alacrán, as he sat down beside Guillermo on the bed and wound an arm around his shoulders.

Alacrán talked to Guillermo for over an hour, explaining that he had been sent over to Italy by La Tía to make quite sure her little nephew didn't take it into his head to tell the police about matters relating to the family. His auntie had forgiven him and was really looking forward to him getting released from prison and returning home to Bogotá. She was going to place him in a high-ranking position within the organization because, one way or another, he had demonstrated that he had cojones. Alacrán then asked Guillermo to tell him the name of his Italian offloader but Guillermo said he didn't know the man's identity.

While Alacrán tried to reassure Guillermo—who didn't believe a word of what he was hearing—Jaramillo went to the toilet, expelled from his rectum a small plastic tube and checked its contents. He then prepared a cup of very sweet coffee which Guillermo, worried only that they would slit his throat, drank without suspecting a thing. A total idiot, mused Alacrán, giving Guillermo a big hug and kissing him on both cheeks. The two new inmates then made their beds and settled down to watch TV.

Guillermo lay wide awake all night and was amazed to be alive the following morning, when Alacrán and Jaramillo were taken to the court. As soon as they were out of sight, Guillermo called the guard and demanded that his compatriots be transferred to another cell block. The guard, however, explained that there was no need, since the two Colombians were sure to be deported as soon as the trial was over.

Arías Cuevas heaved a huge sigh of relief. He had never been so afraid in his life. He slipped on his shoes and went down to the yard for his hour's exercise. After about a quarter of an hour, he felt a bit tired and short of breath, but thought nothing of it. He hadn't closed his eyes all night. He was bound to feel exhausted.

onotto called me on my cell phone. 'A colleague of mine in Venice by the name of Francesco Beltrame, appointed by the court to represent Arías Cuevas, has just phoned me with an excellent piece of news. Cuevas has decided to make a voluntary statement putting Corradi completely in the clear. The investigating magistrate has scheduled a new interview for next week.'

'I'm so pleased to hear that.'

'Of course, I doubt if it's enough to prevent him being indicted, but at the very least it blows a huge hole in the prosecution's case.'

'Right. I think we might call off our investigations for the time being. What do you say?'

'Maybe that would be best. I'll be in touch.'

I waited till the evening to pass on the news to my associates. Sitting in the club at my usual table, we ordered ourselves a round and drank a toast to our success. 'It's always such a pleasure to fuck over the cops,' Rossini commented.

I didn't take Virna home that night. I stayed behind at La Cuccia with Max, drinking, smoking and talking about prison. Every now and then you feel the need to do that. But you have to have been there to understand it.

'It's strange,' I said. 'I've been out for years now but every now and again it still comes back in a rush, flooding my mind like acid. Just when you think you're over it, it kicks in again. Do you know what I mean? They say time helps you forget, but that's bullshit. Prison is still right here with me, like a wedge stuck right in the middle of my life.'

Max the Memory wiped the beer foam from his moustache.

'It's something you're never going to get over, Marco. You didn't reckon with prison the way that I or Old Rossini did. Beniamino has always seen it as an occupational hazard, whereas you ended up in prison by mistake, hauled in during one of their interminable round-ups. And they convicted you even though they knew perfectly well that you were totally innocent of any offence, let alone terrorism. Those days they were just so desperate to crush the movement.'

'What was the worst period for you, Max?'

He smiled bitterly. 'The worst period for me was what they termed Personality Observation. Shrinks, counsellors and social workers, armed with their stupid questionnaires and endless interviews, attempting to find out whether or not prison had "rehabilitated" me.'

I looked him in the eye. 'The way you talk about it, I get the feeling you'll never be over it either.'

'You're right. They forced me into "choosing" to humiliate myself totally, just so I could get out of prison. But what about you? What was the worst time for you?'

'Things were different when I was inside. And in the special prisons, they just laid into us with batons. In those days the screws demanded respect, insisted we refer to them as *superiori*. I could never do that.'

Guillermo's weariness never let up. Quite the reverse. As time went on, he felt weaker and weaker. On the fourth day, he decided he had better go and see the prison doctor and so, in accordance with prison regulations, when the guard did his morning round, Guillermo had his name entered on the list.

Mid-morning he suffered a respiratory collapse. He just managed to bang on the metal panelling of his cell door to alert the guard. But the guard told him to be patient: it wasn't his turn yet. The third time he collapsed he didn't get up again, and so the guard sent for the nurse.

He was still alive when they put him in the ambulance-boat. He died on the Grand Canal, which, despite the freezing weather, was crowded with tourists.

The doctor on duty at the A&E department of the Santissimi Apostoli hospital filled out the death certificate and ordered that the body be transferred to the forensic medicine department for autopsy.

Max, Rossini and I were still sitting at my table when Rossini gently kicked my foot. I turned and saw Bonotto coming towards us. I checked my watch—it was a few minutes before midnight. Max motioned towards the only free chair. The lawyer passed a hand across his face. He seemed upset.

'The Colombian's dead. Murdered. Poisoned.' Bonotto spoke softly so the customers wouldn't hear. 'Rat poison. The police doctor told me they discovered a large amount of Warfarin, the stuff used in rat pellets, in the Colombian's blood. Apparently rats eat them and then die a few hours later. That way, the other rats don't make the connection between the food put down for them and death.'

'A professional job,' Rossini commented.

'That's just what the investigating magistrate said before he ordered Corradi to be thrown into solitary confinement. He's convinced my client wanted to get rid of his principal accuser. And did so.'

'But that doesn't make any sense,' I objected. 'The Colombian was on the point of changing his statement.'

Bonotto threw his arms out wide. 'Was . . . All the judge knows is that Beltrame had requested a fresh interview so the Colombian could place a voluntary statement on the record. For all he knows, Arías Cuevas might have provided further evidence against Corradi.'

Max offered Bonotto a cigarette, but he declined it with a

wave of his hand. 'I assume you've come here for a specific reason, Avvocato,' Max said.

'Sure. We've got to demonstrate right now, before the formal investigation gets under way, that my client had nothing whatsoever to do with this killing. Otherwise I'm going to find myself having to defend him in the High Court on a murder charge. He'd be facing a life sentence. I've already had a word with the governor of Santa Maria Maggiore and he gave me a clear indication that in order to avoid any awkward questions he's considering supporting the Public Prosecutor's case.'

I drank a sip of Calvados. 'We'll clarify the situation as soon as we can. We'll be activating a communication channel that should give us some useful information very fast.'

The lawyer got up and pulled the usual yellow envelope from the inside pocket of his overcoat. 'Okay. I knew I could count on you. I hope you'll have something for me by tomorrow.'

We watched him weave his way rapidly between the tables as he made for the door. 'Well, it certainly wasn't Corradi,' I said, thinking aloud. 'Wasn't the cops either. So who killed the guy?'

'Excellent question,' said Rossini, putting on his overcoat.

'Let's go and have a little chat with Corporal Mansutti. If we hurry, we should find him at the nightclub pawing that girl from Thailand.'

It was a freezing cold night, as black as pitch. The roads were icy but Rossini insisted on driving his powerful and flashy mobster's car with his foot hard down on the floor. 'Someone is playing dirty,' he said, fiddling with his bracelets.

I turned up the heating. 'That's about the only thing we know for sure. The problem is we haven't got the slightest idea as to who or what is driving events. It can't just be police headquarters' appetite for revenge.'

An hour later we pulled into the car-park at the Bulli &
Pupe nightclub in Prata di Pordenone. The bouncer immediately recognized Rossini and insisted on accompanying us in
person to the bar. Rossini stopped a waiter he knew and murmured something in his ear. The waiter nodded and Beniamino
gave me a wink. Mansutti was there all right.

I leaned on the bar as our drinks—on the house, as
always—were poured. I looked around the dance-floor. The
prevailing color was blue. The lighting, calculated to create a
mood of bogus intimacy, made the atmosphere even heavier.
The girls at the tables were all displaying an exaggerated interest in their clients' chit-chat. As I filled my nostrils with the
scent rising from a glass of excellent Calvados, I felt a hand
brush against my wrist.

I turned round to encounter the eyes of a beautiful young
woman looking back at me.

'Hi,' she said.

'Hi.'

'My name's Jana. Want to buy me a drink?'

I took a good look at her. The cone of light from an eyeball
downlighter in the ceiling of the bar lit up one side of her face.
I glanced down at her breasts and then at her legs. The tops of
her hold-ups were peeping out from beneath the hem of her
skirt. I motioned with my thumb to the barman to give her a
drink. He poured her a glass of champagne and passed her a
numbered card, which she slipped into her handbag. When
the bar closed, the cards would be counted and the girls paid
in cash. To the girls, every drink their customer purchased was
worth 10,000 lire. In that kind of business, every little helped.

'My name's Jana,' she said again. 'I'm from Poland. Do you
know Poland?'

I shook my head. I felt a little uneasy but there was nowhere
I could go. Rossini was busy saying hello to a couple of hostesses he knew well, and I would just have to wait till he got

back before I could talk to Mansutti. Meeting the screw at a nightclub was not a wise move, but we were in a hurry to find out precisely what had happened at the prison. There was no time to wait for him outside the usual osteria. I tried to focus on my drink.

'Don't you want to talk?' the Polish girl asked.

'No, I don't. But if you want to have another drink, you can stick around.'

'Solitary type, right? Problems of the heart, no doubt. If you want, we can go somewhere nice and quiet to talk it over.'

Jana was clearly a very determined hostess, the kind that doesn't let go of a client till she has squeezed him dry. I had no choice but to be rude to her and she stalked off, muttering something doubtless unflattering in Polish.

Rossini arrived at long last and beckoned me to follow him. Mansutti was entertaining his new flame in a private booth, and not at all happy to see us. He had one of his hands stuck down the girl's cleavage and left it there as a sort of challenge until Rossini told the girl to leave. She promptly obeyed, and as she edged past I handed her a couple of 50,000 lire notes.

Mansutti wagged a finger at us. 'I know exactly why you're here. But I've got nothing to say about the killing of that Colombian.'

A malicious grin cut across Rossini's face. Moving with lightning speed, he seized Mansutti by the testicles and squeezed hard. The jailer's mouth fell open in pain and surprise. Without making a sound he slid to the floor, curled up in the foetus position, and vomited. Rossini helped him on his way with a couple of powerful punches to the kidneys. Then he settled himself back comfortably, with one of his elegant chamois leather shoes resting on Mansutti's cheek.

We sat and observed Mansutti's contortions for about five minutes. When he had pulled himself together, Rossini yanked him up by the lapels and sat him back down in his chair. The blue lighting accentuated his pallor. One side of his face and hair was covered in vomit and he stank like a drain.

'You're nothing but a slobbering piece of shit,' Rossini reminded him. 'We have a deal and when I snap my fingers I want to see you jump and dance like a performing flea.'

'Please don't hurt me.'

'That's up to you, dickhead.'

I handed Mansutti a glass of fake champagne, which he gulped down thirstily. 'Tell us what happened to the Colombian,' I urged him in a fatherly tone of voice.

'The duty sergeant made the big mistake of assigning to his cell a pair of fellow Colombians who'd been brought in for attempted theft. They're the only ones who could have poisoned him. They were there for just one night. The next day they were tried and deported. The governor wants to cover it all up. Otherwise he, his deputy, and all the daytime officers are in deep shit.'

Rossini and I glanced at each other. 'So they've decided to pin it on Corradi, right?' I asked, even though I already knew the answer.

'Yeah. They've got the backing of Commissario Nunziante so they're feeling pretty relaxed about it,' Mansutti replied.

'Get yourself home,' I told him.

'Please don't tell anybody what I've just told you. If they find out I've talked, I'm finished,' Mansutti begged.

I lit a cigarette. 'Well, we'll have to tell someone about it, but we won't mention your name. You just take it easy, keep a low profile and everything will work out fine.'

We stood up. Before leaving the booth, Rossini turned again to Mansutti, looked him in the eye and hissed, 'Don't ever again show me disrespect.'

Max was waiting for us in his study. He listened carefully to the story Mansutti had told us.

'Let me get this straight. Mansutti is saying that two Colombians had themselves arrested just to get into prison so they could poison a mule. It doesn't add up. Arías Cuevas was small fry. Why put two killers to such trouble? Anyway, if they really were caught red-handed it would be in the papers somewhere.' Max got up and started to thumb through recent copies of *Nuova Venezia*. 'Here it is!' he exclaimed after a couple of minutes, waving a page from the paper at us.

GANG OF SOUTH AMERICANS ARRESTED
AT DEPARTMENT STORE

A professional gang of foreign thieves was arrested yesterday at a department store in Mestre. Pretending not to understand any Italian, they took advantage of the confusion they had created to hide the stolen goods. They are to be tried on a fast-track procedure and deported from Italy, in line with the government's new strategy for combatting foreign racketeers.

Beneath the story the paper carried the mugshots of Alacrán, Jaramillo and their girlfriends.

Max looked at me. 'You need to ask your Paris contact for some information on this. We've got to understand what's going on.'

'You're right.' I looked at my watch. It was just after four in the morning. Too bad. I'd have to wake up Alessio Sperlinga.

'Ciliegia, it's me.'

'For fuck's sake, Alligator. I was fast asleep.'

'Did you get anything?'

'Yeah, I did. I got some photos for you. I was going to send them yesterday but I didn't have the time.'

'Can you do it now?'

'Is it really that urgent?'

'If it wasn't, I wouldn't have woken you up.'

An hour later a page of notes and a couple of photos arrived at Fat Max's email address. He printed everything out and we immediately compared the pictures he had received with the ones in the newspaper. The newspaper mugshot of 'Alberto Jumenez Jamba' matched that of Aurelio Uribe Barragán, aka Alacrán. The notes that Ciliegia's Colombian friends had supplied identified this Alacrán as a hit man belonging to the syndicate run by Rosa Gonzales Cuevas, aka La Tía, a former member of the Medellin cartel currently active in Bogotá. Guillermo Arías Cuevas had been her nephew, but was described as a hanger-on of no importance. Alacrán, on the other hand, was described as a highly dangerous killer. He was believed to have served in the Colombian special forces and to have been sentenced to death by the Colombian guerrillas to avenge the numerous political militants and campesinos he had murdered.

The other photograph matched none of those published in *Nuova Venezia*. It portrayed La Tía in the arms of a young woman.

Old Rossini poured himself a vodka. 'Things are suddenly a lot clearer. Auntie Rosa has had her nephew whacked because she knew he was a piece of trash and might squeal.'

'You have to hand it to them, they've been both cunning and skillful,' Max commented. 'Without running much risk— admittedly with a fair amount of luck on their side—they managed to get close enough to the mule to poison him and then get themselves flown back home courtesy of the Italian police.'

I looked at the photo of the gang leader. 'The problem is, what do we do now? As far as the murder of the mule is concerned, with the information in our possession, Bonotto could probably put Corradi in the clear. But, as for the trafficking charges, we're back where we started. The way things are looking, Corradi will die in jail.'

Rossini yawned. 'We're just going to have to start sifting

through everyone on the scene who deals Colombian coke until we lay our hands on the mule's Italian offloader. We've no other option.'

We all agreed. 'We'll make a start this evening,' Rossini added, as he went out the door.

I slept for a couple of hours, then got up and jumped under the shower. While shaving, I observed my face in the mirror. I didn't like what I saw. I was ageing. I opened the bathroom cabinet and took down a jar of face cream that Virna had given me for Christmas. She must have bought it in some kind of health-food store. It was aimed at men and claimed to have a 'day-and-night anti-wrinkle effect'. I smeared some on my face, massaging gently, as recommended in the instructions. Then I got dressed.

There was a time when I used to dress like a blues singer from Louisiana: garish shirts made of raw silk, blue jeans, and python or alligator boots. Unfortunately, this made me too conspicuous and the cops got me in their sights. In the end I was forced to change my look. I now wore corduroy suits, sea-blue shirts and glove-leather shoes. Virna was in charge of my wardrobe. Every now and then she would drag me along to a store and choose my clothes.

I stepped out of my flat cursing the icy weather and got into my Skoda. Twenty minutes later I parked outside Bonotto's law office. The secretary told him I was waiting to see him and he came out to greet me. His office was tastefully furnished with antique furniture and the walls were decorated with old prints. I told him what we had found out.

'Is your source reliable?' he asked.

'Completely. He's a prison officer at Santa Maria Maggiore. I'm confident that events unfolded precisely as I have described. Unfortunately, I can't give you his name. I'm sure you can imagine the reasons why.'

'Of course, Buratti, of course. I'll go to Venice later this morning and have a word with the prison governor and his deputy. I'm sure we can find a way of safeguarding their careers, while obviating the need for my client to stand trial.'

I lit a cigarette. 'This evening we're going to start making some enquiries among drug dealers, checking out those who sell Colombian cocaine. We want to see if we can identify the mule's Italian contact. It's something of a long shot, but right now we have no other leads. Actually, that's not altogether true. There is one other lead I haven't yet mentioned to you. We thought it best to rule it out right from the outset given that it involves both the police and the Guardia di Finanza.'

The lawyer knit his brows. Before he had time to take offence, I related to him everything that the owner of the Pensione Zodiaco had told us.

'Do you think he could be useful to us if we put him on the stand and cross-examined him?'

I shook my head. 'He doesn't pay his taxes and is terrified of a visit from the Finanza. He'll say whatever the cops want him to say. I'm afraid you can put him down as a hostile witness.'

Bonotto said nothing for a couple of minutes. Then he suddenly thumped the table. 'I can't make any damn sense of all the comings and goings of the investigators at the hotel. I have to tell you, Buratti, this case has got me really worried. I've always steered clear of defending drug dealers and as a result have no experience in this kind of trial. Any mistake I make could ruin Corradi's chances.'

I shrugged. It was time for some plain speaking. 'Venice Police headquarters have received hard information to the effect that your client did in fact kill the two cops outside the jeweler's shop in Caorle. This is the real nub of it. If Corradi goes to trial on these trafficking charges, you can bet your life that some high-ranking official or other will slip the court judges the information on the killing just before they retire to consider their verdict, and Corradi will get the maximum sentence. The only way we can save him is if we turn up some really incontrovertible evidence of his innocence, leaving the judge no choice but to release him. In Italy, as you said yourself, trials are won or lost at the investigation stage. After that, it's too late.'

Bonotto looked troubled. He removed his glasses and cleaned them with a white handkerchief. 'I was so sure he was innocent. I defended him with passion . . .'

'It was my duty to inform you, Avvocato. Does it change anything, now that you know?'

'No, it doesn't. The evidence brought against him was entirely circumstantial. Besides, as a lawyer, it's my job to defend my client to the best of my ability.'

'Will you still defend him with the same passion as before?'

Bonotto sighed. 'Yes, I will. I'd much rather he wasn't guilty of a double murder. Those men had families. And besides, Corradi lied to me. He swore on the heads of his dead parents that he was innocent.'

'That was another bad mistake. One should never lie to one's own defense lawyer. Listen. If you don't feel up to defending him, drop the case.'

'I can't do that. I'll defend him. But it's the last time.'

I got up and shook his hand.

That evening we began to scour the nightclubs, lap-dance joints, discotheques, cafés, and bars of every description in and around Venice. We very quickly realized we were hunting for the proverbial needle in a haystack.

Whereas heroin was now the drug of the most desperate, marginalized section of society, most users of cocaine and ecstasy-like synthetic substances were pretty ordinary people leading pretty ordinary lives, and their use of drugs was essentially recreational. Coke in particular had become really popular. The world was full of fine upstanding people who somehow felt the need to get out of their heads at weekends. Dealers had no trouble at all selling coke because buyers were prepared to go out of their way to get hold of it.

It was an amazing money-spinner, expanding day by day. We came across business people, sales assistants, young factory workers, all with their pockets stuffed with cash, purchasing coke from big-mouthed wealthy dealers. We recognized quite a few of them from prison and got talking. They told us how things had changed with the arrival of the new foreign-based mafias. The entire market was spiralling out of control. Russians, Nigerians, Croats, the Neapolitan Camorra, the Sicilian Mafia: they had all carved out a slice of the action. And there were the independents, springing up like mushrooms from nowhere at all. Nobody was chasing them any longer. It wasn't like the days when the local Brenta Mafia ran things.

Antonio Soldan, nicknamed Zanza, a former con-artist who had thrown everything he had into coke dealing, was in the mood to talk. 'Right now . . . say your company's in a spot of trouble, or you fancy opening a shop, or there's something you're hankering after, like you want to treat yourself to a boat, or something . . . you take a trip to Bolivia or Colombia, buy some coke, put it in a condom, stick it up your lady's fanny, and you're away.'

Like everyone else, Soldan had no idea who Arías Cuevas' buyer could have been. 'It's almost certainly an independent operator or even some completely new channel. The way things are now, it's anybody's guess.'

In a salsa and merengue dance-club, we bumped into Victoria, Corradi's woman. She was with three Colombian hostesses who had a night off and were out to have a good time. We joined them at their table. Victoria was feeling sorry for herself and had had a glass too many. 'They didn't let me see Nazzareno. They said he was in solitary.'

I laid my hand on her arm. 'In a couple of days, you'll be able to go and visit him, you'll see. Just this morning, his lawyer went along to the prison to have a word with the governor.'

Victoria's lips curled. 'That lawyer! He isn't doing anything for Nazzareno. All he knows how to do is ask for money.'

Until he overheard this remark, Rossini had been talking and joking with the other girls, but he now weighed in hard.

'Go home and go to bed. You're beginning to talk crap. It sure as hell wasn't his lawyer that put your man behind bars.'

I looked at Rossini. 'Leave her alone.'

'Look. This lady's man is in prison. She's got to learn how to behave. If she carries on like this, sooner or later it'll affect Nazzareno.'

I let it go. Rossini was a gangster of the old school. He took the view that the need to abide by certain rules extended to prisoners' family members.

We got up and left the club, having decided we had spent enough time nosing around among drug dealers for one night. We went back to La Cuccia. It had already closed and I was relieved to discover that Virna had gone home. We knocked on Max's door. 'I was expecting you,' he said, handing us a couple of glasses, Calvados and vodka.

'How did it go?' he asked.

'Badly,' I replied. I gave him a quick summary of our investigations, concluding with an account of the way Rossini had laid into Corradi's woman.

'It'll have done her nothing but good,' Rossini growled. 'How many kids in prison have we seen go out of their minds before trial because their girlfriends or mothers and fathers put it into their heads that their lawyers are not defending them properly? They end up doing something stupid, like insulting a screw, and pick up a conviction for defamation or, worse, get knifed in the back during a brawl.'

Max glanced at me and shrugged. 'Rossini's right, damn it. A prisoner's mental balance is a delicate thing, especially just before trial.'

'Look,' I snorted, 'right now I don't particularly want to get bogged down in the intricate psychology of prisoners awaiting trial. I'd rather we decided how to proceed with this investigation. We can't waste any more evenings on wild goose chases.'

Max switched on his computer. He had dug out all the articles from the local press on investigations into Colombian cocaine trafficking and saved them in a file.

'The only interesting snippet I came across relates to the arrest of a schoolteacher in a discotheque in Dolo, near Venice.' An article from *Nuova Venezia*, published a couple of months previously, came up on the screen.

SCHOOLTEACHER ARRESTED WHILE SELLING
COCAINE TO CHILDREN IN DISCO—EDUCATION AUTHORITY
CONVENES EMERGENCY SESSION

From classroom to cell block in a matter of hours, all thanks to the Carabinieri!

Annibale Tavan, 42, a math and science teacher at the Sandro Pertini secondary school in Chioggia, was arrested yesterday at a discotheque in Gaia di Dolo where he was caught selling cocaine. During the week, Tavan was a respected schoolteacher, above all suspicion. But on Saturday nights, he allegedly turned into a drug dealer, selling top-quality cocaine and ecstasy to children little older than those he taught in class. The arrest was the result of prompt action taken by the Carabinieri of Chioggia.

The article continued with statements from Carabiniere officers, Tavan's staffroom colleagues and some of the parents of his students. Max had underlined in red the section of the article that was of most interest for our investigations: 'The Carabinieri are now looking for Tavan's supplier. So far their enquiries indicate that Tavan has not travelled abroad at all in the last four years.'

I poured myself some Calvados. 'What makes you think this is worth following up?'

Max scratched his paunch with his fingertips. 'It's just possible that the schoolteacher gave the cops a tip-off, enabling them to arrest the Colombian at the airport. It's only a hunch, but none of the other investigations covered by the press are of any interest at all.'

I turned to Rossini. 'What do you think?'

'It's worth a try,' he answered.

I moved back to the computer screen and read the article through again, taking my time. Alongside the report of the arrest, there was an interview with the man in charge of drugs rehab programmes in Mestre:

COCAINE NOW THE MOST POPULAR DRUG—
9% OF ALL SCHOOL STUDENTS IN MESTRE
SAY THEY HAVE TRIED IT

Cocaine use is now extremely widespread among young people throughout our region. We are very concerned that increasing numbers of teenagers are becoming regular cocaine users. It's cheap and easily available on the streets. Second only to cocaine in popularity are ecstasy and the so-called new drugs. With these substances, kids are playing a kind of Russian roulette, often taking them precisely because they don't know what their effect will be. In reality their effect depends essentially on the kind of substance that the chemists playing around with the basic compound arrive at.

And it's a race against time. The moment a substance

gets classified as a drug and placed on the prohibited list, the producers come up with a new one kids feel they have to try. Taking 'E' is becoming a highly risky business now that its manufacture is increasingly in the hands of East European chemists. There is no way of knowing what kind of ingredients they use.

An idea flashed through my mind but failed to take solid shape, dissolving almost instantly in a mix of alcohol and tiredness.

'I'm going to bed,' I announced.

Rossini gave me an affectionate slap on the cheek. 'I'll pick you up after lunch. Make sure you're awake.'

To find out who had supplied the schoolteacher with cocaine, we agreed that the first thing to do was pay a visit to the man in charge of security at the Gaia di Dolo discotheque where Tavan had been arrested. Most chief bouncers are police informants and, according to the information Rossini had gathered that morning, Giovanni Scrivo was no exception. As a former security guard and one-time kickboxing champion, by the age of forty Scrivo was tired of risking his life standing around outside banks and had turned instead to the lush pastures of nightclub security.

We drove to his house, an anonymous little villa not far from Mira with a panoramic view over the chemical works at Miralanza. His wife, a charming and discreet Filipino, opened the door to us, then called her husband and disappeared. We stood by the open door and waited for a few minutes until Scrivo arrived, barefoot, in nothing but a pair of jeans, displaying a powerful chest and arms the size of Parma hams.

He scrutinized us with expert care. 'What can I do for you?' he asked, planting his feet squarely on the floor.

Rossini leaned on the door jamb and calmly lit a cigarette.

Maybe Karate Kid didn't scare him, but he sure scared the wits out of me. From that distance he could kickbox me in the teeth before I had a clue what was happening. I summoned up all my courage. 'We figure it was you who gave Tavan to the cops. We don't give a shit about it. It's none of our business,' I quickly added, to reassure him. 'What we're after is the name of the individual who supplied the school-teacher with Colombian coke. You must know who it was. It's got to be another of the regulars at the discotheque. What's more, it's reasonable to assume you've sold him to the police too. And, since the papers haven't carried any news about his arrest, he must have skipped out just in time.'

The bouncer stared at Rossini. 'Are you going to leave here on your own legs or must I tell my wife to call a couple of ambulances?'

I snapped my fingers to regain Scrivo's attention. 'This here is Beniamino Rossini. If you lay a finger on him, he'll come back and shoot you.'

Scrivo nodded slowly. 'I've heard of you. From Milan, right? There's a rumour going round that you're the guy that killed Tristano Castelli's soldiers last year.'

Rossini gave him an ugly grin. 'Yeah, I've heard those rumours.'

Scrivo scratched his densely carpeted chest, lost in thought. 'It'll cost you.'

I pulled a couple of 50,000 lire notes from the inside pocket of my jacket. The bouncer quickly stuffed them into his jeans. 'The guy's name is Fernando Maiorino. He lives not far from here, at Spinea. Since the schoolteacher was arrested, Maiorino's been missing, evading arrest. But his business is all concentrated in this area so he won't have gone far.'

'Is that it?' I asked.

'Well, as it happens, I do have another piece of information.'

I pulled out another two notes. 'Is it worth hearing?'

Scrivo shrugged. 'Let's just say you're not the only people looking for Maiorino. As well as the police, obviously.'

I handed him the money.

'The other evening, this lady showed up at the discotheque. South American, about fifty, with a young girl in tow. She paid me in dollars to tell her the name of Tavan's supplier, and then asked for a list of other people who peddle Colombian coke.'

Rossini and I exchanged glances. I had the photos of Alacrán and La Tía in my pocket. I showed Scrivo the photo of La Tía.

'Yeah, that's her. It's not the same girl though. This one's a blonde and she's uglier and fatter.'

'It would be best if you didn't report any part of this conversation to the cops,' Rossini advised in a flat tone of voice.

'Then I won't,' said Scrivo. 'I wouldn't want to end up like Castelli's men.' He turned his back on us and closed the door.

'So La Tía is still around,' I said, getting into the car.

Rossini started the engine. 'Right. She's obviously looking for her nephew's offloader so she can go into business with him.'

'Do you reckon it's Maiorino?'

'Hard to say. Even if at first sight he seems a likely candidate.'

'What are we going to do? Try and track La Tía via the dealer?'

'That's far too long and complicated. If she's holed up somewhere in the Colombian community, she shouldn't be so hard to locate.'

It was a Colombian hostess working at the Diana nightclub in the small town of Mansuè, near Treviso, who put us on the right track to discovering La Tía's hiding-place. One night at work she had been talking to a cousin of hers who said she had overheard another Colombian hostess saying that a lady from Bogotá with links to the narcos had arrived in the area. The girl who had mentioned this fact was staying at Da Gianna, a cheap hotel in Jesolo regularly used by Colombian hostesses from the specific Bogotá barrio over which La Tía reigned supreme. The girl at the Diana advised us to steer clear of the lady in question and begged us not to inform any of her fellow-countrywomen that she had supplied us information regarding La Tía's whereabouts. This cost us 100,000 lire and a couple of gin and tonics.

Da Gianna turned out to be virtually identical to Pensione Zodiaco where Corradi had been arrested: tacky Sixties furnishings, family atmosphere, and full board for just 80,000 lire. The only real difference was that during the quieter winter months Signora Gianna, the landlady, let rooms to Colombian girls and didn't take too much interest in nighttime comings and goings.

Doing business with Signora Gianna was a pleasure. She was much more affable and less timorous than her fellow hotelier at the Zodiaco. Short, chubby and sixtyish, she wore a dress with a reckless neckline. On her head she had a huge chignon from which several ringlets escaped to decorate her temples. Her face was rather heavily made-up.

Old Rossini paraded the gallant smile that he reserved for special occasions. 'Bella Signora,' he began, 'we are enquiring after two Colombian lady friends. One is about fifty and the other about twenty . . .'

Signora Gianna studied the numerous rings on her finger and checked her perfectly varnished nails. 'Signora Luisa Teresa Fonseca Trompiez and Signorina Alexandra Nieto Bernal. A pair of puffed-up dykes.'

'That's them.'

The landlady assumed an air of impertinence. 'I would need to look at the register. For all I know, they may have checked out by now.'

I placed some 50,000 lire notes on the reception desk.

'They're still here but right now they're out,' she said in a matter-of-fact voice, pocketing the money.

'We'd like to wait for them in their rooms, give them a little surprise,' Rossini suggested.

Signora Gianna sighed. 'Well, you certainly don't look like the police. You're not intending to make any trouble in my hotel, are you?'

Rossini took her chin gently between two fingers. 'None at all, Bella Signora, just a little chat between friends.'

'Another fifty thousand each and I'll show you upstairs.'

I paid without a murmur and Signora Gianna led the way, tripping lightly on her high-heeled gold-painted sandals.

The room's furniture consisted of a double bed, a wardrobe, a table, two chairs, a minibar and a TV. We made a rapid but thorough search. All we found was a roll of dollars hidden in the leg of a chair. We made ourselves comfortable on the bed and watched the eight o'clock news. And that was the way the two women found us when they opened their door.

We heard the key turning in the lock but went on watching TV anyway. They were showing a particularly interesting report on the cluster bombs that NATO forces had left scattered around in the Adriatic Sea during their war on Serbia. The navy was insisting the whole area had been cleared but fishermen kept finding the lethal yellow devices in their nets. 'It seems they upset the cuttlefish. It'll be a lean year in the fishing ports,' Rossini informed me with the air of a know-all.

By this time, La Tía and Aisa had come into the room and were closing the door behind them. The girl was holding a long hairpin in her hand. There was no doubt at all in my mind that she knew how to use it.

Half in Italian and half in Spanish, Rosa Gonzales Cuevas asked us who we were and what we wanted, and thus began a curious conversation in a mixture of both languages.

'Hola, Tía,' I greeted her. 'That was a neat job Alacrán did for you in that prison. Though having your nephew murdered can't be too pleasant.'

La Tía took a chair and pulled it up to the side of the bed. I hauled myself into a sitting position, and Rossini did the same. Aisa stayed close to the door.

'You could be Colombian cops, I suppose, but you are certainly not Italian ones,' La Tía observed. 'So who are you?'

'We're trying to find your nephew's Italian contact. A man has been wrongfully imprisoned in his place and the mistake needs to be rectified as soon as possible.'

La Tía's face contorted with disappointment. 'I was hoping you were the offloader. Or that you might want to do business.'

'Could Maiorino be the guy we're after?' I asked mischievously, just to let her know we were aware of her reasons for remaining in Italy.

'No, it's not him. I was talking to him today. He's involved in a different racket. He doesn't deal in Colombian coke at all, but in low-grade Bolivian product.'

Rossini clapped briefly. 'Congratulations, you did well to find him.'

La Tía gave him a sly smile. 'It was easy. Everyone here likes South American girls and everyone talks to everyone else. He is hiding in the apartment of a Dominican chica who is snorting her way through all his reserves of coke. He is a cretin. It won't be long before they find him.'

La Tía told Aisa to bring her a drink. Aisa fetched a half-litre bottle of Blanco from a suitcase. Doña Rosa unscrewed the cap and took a long pull before handing us the bottle. The smell of aniseed flooded the room. I declined the offer, passing the bottle to Rossini, who took a long swig.

'What shall we do? Kill each other or do business?' La Tía asked.

Old Rossini got to his feet. 'You deserve to die and be buried at sea in an elegant pair of concrete shoes.'

La Tía yawned and lit a cigarette. 'Ah, cut the crap. My nephew had it coming. He was a weakling. Sooner or later he would have talked. Look, I have a business proposal to put to you.'

'Drugs and drug dealers are not our line of work,' I pointed out.

'That makes no difference. How do you reckon I knew Maiorino wasn't the right man?'

I shrugged. 'I guess you had some information about the real contact.'

'Precisely. Which means that I'm the only one who can help you find who you're looking for.'

Rossini took the bottle out of her hand. 'What do you want in return?'

'Other information.'

'Of what kind?'

'The girls have given me a list of dealers. I want to know which I can trust. I haven't got the time to find out for myself which ones work for the police.'

'Why don't you look for your nephew's offloader and deal direct with him?' I asked, genuinely puzzled.

She smoothed her skirt down. 'Because he was the one who persuaded that idiot nephew of mine to try ripping me off. I could never trust him.'

'So you're planning to open up a supply route to Italy?' Rossini asked.

'Coke sells like crazy here. There's great business to be done.'

I decided to put out some feelers. 'What if we decide to screw you?'

Doña Rosa threw her arms out wide in exasperation. 'How can we possibly come to an agreement if you gentlemen continue to threaten me?'

'The lady's right, Marco,' Rossini said. 'At bottom, all we'd be trading is information.'

La Tía waved her hand at Aisa who swivelled around, hitched up her skirt and removed a piece of paper hidden in her panties. The list of dealers was passed from hand to hand till it reached my associate.

Rossini glanced down the list. 'I know some of them. Two of them are definitely informants.'

Doña Rosa smiled with satisfaction. 'How long will it take you to check all the names?'

'A couple of days,' Rossini replied calmly.

'Fine. In ten days maximum I plan to return to Colombia. That is when our tourist visas run out.'

Rossini's tone of voice hardened sharply. 'Your turn now.' La Tía shook her head. 'No, I don't think so. You give me the list and I'll tell you how to find your man.'

The argument dragged on for at least ten minutes but there was no getting around her. She simply refused to budge.

'Vile bitch,' Rossini muttered, as we left the hotel.

'Are you planning to stick to the agreement?' I asked.

'Of course. Double-crossing La Tía won't put a stop to cocaine dealing. Besides, she's so accustomed to mistrusting people that she's sure to do her own investigations. And if she discovers we've slipped her a bum name, we won't get anything out of her.'

'I still don't like it.'

'Come on, Marco, don't jerk me around. I've seen you go for worse trade-offs in the past.'

Rossini drove me back to La Cuccia. He was going to take personal charge of gathering the information La Tía wanted on the dealers. Then he would come back and pick me up so we could go together to our next meeting with her.

It was dinner time so I decided to invite myself over to Max's. I found him with a rolling-pin in his hand, busily rolling out dough to prepare pappardelle, which he was planning to cook in a stock with chicken livers. On the kitchen table a book-rest held a recipe book of Venetian cuisine entitled *Dining with the Doges*, open at the dish Max was intent on preparing. Next to the book-rest stood a bottle of Bardolino Superiore, the wine that the book's authors recommended to accompany the meal. In the background, the latest CD by Ivano Fossati, a singer-songwriter of Max's and my generation.

> *I never betrayed my youth*
> *I don't have to prove my innocence*
> *I'm guilty at the very most*
> *Of love and similar deviations*
> *Such as melancholy*
> *Such as nostalgia . . .*

Max the Memory had been forced to lie low for many years and cooking had been a good way of getting through long days spent on his own. Marielita, his woman, usually arrived home late from working as a street musician. She was murdered while he was in prison and when he got out again he went on living as if still in hiding.

He rarely ventured out, and never in the evening. At most, he would come down to the club, spend a few hours there, then go back upstairs to his flat and shut himself away with his books, his music, his films, his files and the internet. One day I turned to him and said, 'You're always cooped up here. Why don't you get out . . . go to the cinema . . .?'

He just stood there, his hands resting as always on his beer gut, looking at me with those big faded-blue eyes of his.

'People recognize me, Marco, and I can't stand sidelong glances and remarks muttered behind my back. I bump into old political comrades, the ones who jumped ship just in the nick of time and the ones who somehow always had the best possible reason for turning their back on the movement. We greet one another with embarrassment, our eyes looking elsewhere . . . I would rather watch a video.'

'If that's how it is, why don't you just leave this town, this country, altogether?'

'Maybe I will one day. But right now, like you, I'd rather be here than anywhere else. And for exactly the same reason. It's on account of the investigations I do, the cases we work on together, the bits and pieces of truth we uncover, the little skirmishes we have with the corrupt and powerful. It's the engine that keeps both our lives going. It's what makes sense of everything.'

'I guess you're right, Max. Except that I have no urge to leave. I can't imagine living anywhere else.'

'Perhaps one day we'll be forced to leave in a hurry.'

'Why?'

'Because our investigations are illegal, because our methods our illegal, and because on more than one occasion Old Rossini has pulled out his gun to save our skins. So far we've got away with it, but the first wrong move we make we're in deep shit.'

I observed my friend as he moved easily among his pots and pans. It seemed to me that all this activity was just a way of giving time a little meaning, safe from the outside world. But then it struck me that I had no right to judge him. I got up and walked over to his living room to fetch the bottle of Calvados.

While we ate, I told Max about the meeting with La Tía. Max then went back over the entire case, point by point, examining our investigative strategy. As an analyst, Max was a genius, and it was fascinating to hear him talk.

Halfway through dinner my cell phone rang. It was Bonotto informing me he had reached an agreement with the prison governor and that Corradi had already been released from solitary and returned to the cell block. They had decided to incriminate the actual killers, the two Colombians who, according to the story they had concocted, had somehow supplied their compatriot with poisoned food with the help of an unsuspecting Albanian cell-sweeper who, in the meantime, like the two Colombians, had been freed from prison and deported. I complimented Bonotto on his work. All in all, it was a pretty plausible reconstruction and it involved nobody but prisoners.

I kept Max company while he washed the dishes and then went downstairs to the club. I wanted to see Virna but as soon as I walked in, Rudy Scanferla, the club manager, came up to me. 'We've got to take a look at the books, Marco. Would tomorrow afternoon suit you?'

'Sure. How's business?'

'Good. We've got some pretty loyal customers now and the takings are steady and good.'

I looked around and felt a glow of satisfaction that this club was mine. People were smoking and drinking, having a good time listening to Eloisa Deriu, who was just then paying tribute to Billie Holiday, singing one of Lady Day's greatest numbers, 'God Bless the Child.'

> . . . *Mama may have*
> *Papa may have*
> *But God bless the child*
> *That's got his own!*
> *That's got his own!*

I closed my eyes. For a second I imagined I was in the Ebony Club on 52nd street. The audience called out for another Billie Holiday number and our resident singer obliged them with 'Fine and Mellow.'

Without making a noise Virna came up behind me, stood on tiptoes and kissed me on the neck. 'I thought you'd vanished.'

'I've been avoiding you the last couple of days.'

'Afraid of heavy talk?'

'Uh-huh.'

'Will you come and sleep at my place tonight?'

'I'd love to.'

'I've missed you.'

'Me too.'

I sat down at my table. After a while, Max arrived and began looking around to see if there were any girls he might try to pick up. 'I feel like falling in love,' he said, with a chuckle.

I pointed to a table where three young women were engaged in light-hearted banter. 'That brunette in the middle is really nice-looking,' I said.

'I prefer the one that's just walked in.'

I turned to look. 'You've got good taste, Max, but she's not available. That's Nazzareno Corradi's woman.'

Victoria picked her way through the room to our table, attracting the appreciative stares of every man in the club. She was wearing a long coat left unbuttoned. At each step she took it fell open to reveal a leather miniskirt with a chunky golden zip up the middle, and a pair of fantastic legs.

'Bonotto told me I'd find you here. May I sit down?'

I pointed to the chair beside me. 'What are you drinking, Victoria?'

'Bourbon. With ice and water.'

I called Virna, who took the order without taking her eyes off Victoria for a second. Jealousy spurted from her every pore.

Victoria used my cigarette lighter. 'I came to say sorry for the other evening. I'd been drinking and was feeling sad.'

I placed a hand on her arm. Generally I keep my hands to myself, but Victoria had the power to confuse me. 'Don't worry about it,' I said. 'Nothing happened. My friend is just a little old-fashioned.'

'He was right, though. I hoped I might find him here and apologize to him too.'

'He's not here this evening, but I'll pass on your message. As you can see, Bonotto is a good lawyer. He knows what he's doing. Thanks to him, the murder charge has been dropped and Nazzareno is no longer in solitary.'

Victoria smiled. 'I'm going to visit him tomorrow. At last I'll see him.'

When Virna arrived with the tray of drinks, my hand was still on Victoria's arm. She shot me a look of pure poison. I was going to have some explaining to do. She went off to wait on other tables.

Victoria raised her glass. 'I miss Nazzareno more and more. Is there any hope he'll be out soon?' Her eyes filled with tears. The way Max was looking at me, I felt I had no choice but to try and reassure her.

'It's an awkward case,' I began to explain. 'Your man has police headquarters gunning for him. They're doing all they can to frame him. Right now, we've got nothing concrete to put him in the clear, but we're following up a couple of leads that may well give us something we can work with.'

Her eyes lit up. 'What have you found out?'

I shook my head. 'For the time being, there's nothing I can tell you.'

Victoria got up and shook our hands. 'I would like to thank you for everything you're doing for Nazzareno,' she said.

'That's some woman,' said Max. 'There should be a few more bombshells like that wandering through this joint.'

'That's not such a good idea,' I replied. 'Bombshells like that attract a type of male clientele that I don't wish to see at La Cuccia.'

At half past four I drove to Padova, following Virna's car along icy deserted roads. The fields on either side of the main road were covered with thick frost. Even in the city center, there was no one stirring.

We made love slowly and for a long time. Virna was in great

need of tenderness. As I smoked my last cigarette before going to sleep I told her I would like to go away with her somewhere, just the two of us. For a weekend, say. She weighed my words in silence.

'It's the first time you've come up with anything so romantic. I have to say the idea attracts me, even if a weekend is a long time. I'm not sure you can play the lover for more than a couple of hours at a stretch.'

I could hardly blame her. Still, I pretended to be wounded by her lack of faith. 'Think it over,' I said, to end the conversation. 'You can take your time. Right now I've got to finish this investigation.'

'Is the bimbo you were caressing tonight a key element in the case?'

'There's no need to be catty, Virna. Her man's in prison. I was just trying to comfort her a little.'

'I never realized a private investigator's job description included that type of service.'

Somehow I couldn't take that in silence. We had a row.

Ten minutes later I was back in my car, heading home. I stopped off at a bar that I knew sold Calvados, not far from the covered market. I was intending to have just one and then go straight home to bed but I bumped into a couple of transvestites I had known for years and who were keen to talk. They told me how hard street-work had become since the Albanians had gained control of the racket, and then they related a whole series of amusing anecdotes about their clients. I didn't get home till midday. Just in time to grab a couple of hours sleep before Rossini came to pick me up. We were going to see La Tía.

Doña Rosa and Aisa had been out shopping. They were parading up and down in clothes and footwear by top Italian designers. Aisa had a split lip. The wound was recent and she kept running her tongue over it. I glanced at La Tía's hands. On the ring-finger of her right hand she wore a large Colombian emerald mounted on white gold. She noticed my glance and felt obliged to explain that she had caught Aisa flirting with a shop assistant. Aisa burst into tears and ran off into the bathroom.

Doña Rosa looked at us conspiratorially. 'The little tramp is beginning to tire me. Sooner or later . . .'

'We don't give a shit about your aching heart,' Old Rossini hissed.

La Tía pretended she hadn't heard. 'Did you bring the list?' My associate had concealed it in a cigarette packet, which he now handed over. 'The names underlined in red are police informants. Those in black are mid-to-high level dealers. The others are all nobodies.'

La Tía extracted the piece of paper and stuck it in her bra. It was her turn now. 'Guillermo met the man you're looking for in Bogotá, in a high-class whorehouse. He was there to find a girl he could take to Tokyo and put to work in Pleasure City . . .'

I raised a hand to interrupt her. 'What's all this about Japan?'

'The Japanese are crazy about our girls, but it's hard to get them into the country. Japanese immigration makes a lot of fuss about illnesses, vaccinations and, well, drug trafficking.'

But if the girls arrive in the company of some European or other, and if they can prove they've spent some time in the West, then everything's much more straightforward. Naturally, you need the right contacts.'

'Yakuza, the Japanese mafia,' Rossini muttered.

'Sure. They're the ones in control of the brothels.'

'Who pays for the girls?' I asked, my curiosity aroused.

'The Japanese brothel-owner pays one half and the Colombian prostitution ring the other. It's fifty thousand dollars per girl. But it's quickly recouped, with the girl herself sending seventy per cent of her earnings back home each month.'

'And what if she doesn't?' I asked.

'They all have families,' La Tía explained, running an index finger across her throat.

Old Rossini opened the minibar and took out a miniature bottle of vodka. 'Why didn't you get the people who run the whorehouse in Bogotá to give you the Italian's name? They must know him.'

'I didn't want the whole of Bogotá knowing someone had stolen nearly a kilo of coke off me. They might get the idea I was no longer able to run my business.'

I motioned to her to continue.

'It was the fifth girl the Italian had taken to the Far East. Anyway, he met Guillermo and suggested that instead of distributing the coke around Bogotá, like he was supposed to, he could smuggle it into Italy. The idea was for Guillermo to do the trip, return home, pay me the amount I was expecting, and pocket the difference. Coke costs ten times as much here as in Colombia.'

'Right,' I said. 'Is that it?'

'Is that it?' she repeated. 'How many Italians are there living in the Veneto region who traffic Colombian girls to Japan?'

She was right. It was a good lead. It was just that neither I nor my associate had ever heard of this particular line of business. The man we were looking for had to be a freelancer, working on his own. He might not be that easy to identify.

Old Rossini threw his empty vodka miniature into the waste-basket. 'Why didn't you question the Colombian girls who work in the clubs around here?'

'Like I said before, I don't want people to know I got ripped off.'

He was unconvinced. 'Then how come you tried so hard to find your nephew's offloader?'

'I can assure you that if I had managed to lay my hands on the son of a bitch, he wouldn't have gone around shouting about it.'

To make her meaning clear, La Tía reached behind her back and extracted from the seam of her dress a hairpin just like the one Aisa had threatened us with the first time we had met. It was about twenty centimeters long and its handle consisted of a ball of amber. As on the previous occasion, I had no doubt as to their ability to murder Guillermo's contact. It would have been a quick, clean job. A blow straight to the heart or through an eye and into the brain.

The conversation was at an end. It was time to go. 'I'm leaving in exactly eight days,' La Tía said. 'If you need me, you know where I am.'

As we strolled past the reception desk, Signora Gianna winked at us. 'All the gorgeous chicks in this place and you two waste your time on that pair of dykes.'

'If I only could, I'd waste a little time with you, Bella Signora,' Rossini replied.

We walked through the fog to a well stocked wine bar. I asked the owner to mix me an Alligator, specifying as always the precise ingredients and measures as well as the origin of the cocktail. My associate ordered a glass of Prosecco and some sandwiches.

'Can you call Mansutti, Beniamino? Tomorrow I want to talk to Nazzareno.'

The bent prison guard answered at once. Rossini gave him his orders and then listened patiently. 'Okay, you can go back to the Thai chick. And if you behave yourself, I'll see you get a reward,' Rossini reassured him.

'Any problems?' I asked.

'None. He just asked me for permission to go back to the nightclub.'

'What do we do now?'

'We search for our man. We've got a physical description: fiftyish, large build, light brown hair. And we know he's involved in a very particular kind of trade.'

'I guess we could start with Victoria, then.'

'You really like her, don't you?'

'Yes, I do,' I replied simply. 'She's sweet and lovely. Just the way I like them.'

'There are some things you shouldn't even think about. Her man's behind bars.'

'Don't start with your nagging. I just like looking at her, that's all. You know perfectly well I'd never go after a prison widow.'

Rossini took a bite from his asparagus sandwich. 'Don't take offence, but when it comes to the ladies you've always been a total innocent. Just look at the way you behave with Virna. She'll end up dumping you and then, as usual, you'll come crying on my shoulder like a bullcalf.'

'That's not going to happen. You'll see,' I snapped.

'What's not going to happen? Her dumping you or you coming and crying on my shoulder?'

I got up and went to pay the bill.

The journey to Ormelle was even longer than usual. Owing

to an accident near the turn-off for San Donà di Piave a long tailback had formed, obliging us to crawl along at walking pace for over an hour. A Slovenian semi had sailed through the central crash barrier hitting an oncoming Peugeot 206 with two young men on board. They had just got out of the bicycle factory where they worked Mondays to Fridays.

'No clubbing for them this week,' Rossini muttered wrily.

I lit my umpteenth cigarette and took a sip from the bottle of Calvados I had purchased at the liquor store. 'You know somehow it never occurs to me that I might die in a road accident,' I said, thinking aloud.

Rossini touched his bracelets nervously. He didn't like that kind of talk. 'Me neither. And as long as I'm at the wheel, don't worry, it's not going to happen.'

I rang the bell at Corradi's house. The fog was so thick you couldn't see the front door from the gate.

Victoria welcomed us with a shy smile and showed us into the lounge. The television was on. One of the state-owned channels was showing an Italian soap.

Rossini got straight to the point. 'Have you ever heard of an Italian who takes girls from Colombia to Japan?'

She shook her head. 'No, I haven't. Ever since I arrived in Italy, I've only ever worked at the Black Baron club in Eraclea. I've never done any kind of hostess work so I know nothing about the kind of business where girls go to bed with their customers.'

'Do you know any Colombian girls who might be able to give us the information we're looking for?'

'No, I don't. I've never heard of anything like that. Are you sure you've got it right? Maybe it's a lie.'

I got to my feet. 'You could be right. But given the situation we're in right now, we have to check everything out, even the tiniest little clue.'

At the front door, Rossini stopped and wheeled around.

'One more question. Do you think Nazzareno might know anything?'

'I really doubt it. But I'll be seeing him next week, so I can ask.'

I shut the gate behind us. 'You asked her that just to see whether Corradi has told her anything about Mansutti and the cell phone, right?'

'Yeah. It's not that I don't trust him. But we can't be too careful.'

'For this evening, we're through.'

Old Rossini looked at his watch. 'It's ten past nine. I promised Sylvie I'd take her out to dinner and then drive her over to the club around eleven. I guess I have no choice but to invite you along.'

Sylvie was living not far from Ormelle, in a hotel. She was pleased to see me, and I thought she looked fantastic. She was an extremely sensual woman, and when she did her belly-dancing she drove men quite literally mad. Including me. When she was performing, I liked to hang around, completely drunk, and just watch her dance. My imagination would run wild, venturing into previously unexplored territory. It was one of the few things I had never mentioned to Beniamino.

Rossini embraced her, kissed her and murmured something amorous in her ear. She laughed, throwing her head way back. Any number of local industrialists and businessmen had attempted to seduce her, but for the last couple of years Sylvie had been in love with Rossini. It was a very easy-going relationship: they lived a day at a time and were both well aware it wouldn't last forever.

Over dinner, she made an unsuccessful attempt to discover what the two of us were up to. It was just a harmless game with her. She had grown up in the nightclub scene and knew the rules. After the meal, I watched her admiringly as she poured two spoonfuls of honey into a triple grappa, then downed the lot in a single gulp. 'It's what gives me the energy,' she told me. Then we drove her to her nightclub, a high-class joint in San Polo di Piave. She asked us if we wanted to stay and watch her perform. I was tempted to say yes, but I couldn't afford a skinful that night. I needed to be lucid the next day. Besides, I had a hunch that Rossini didn't want me hanging around.

The temperature had dropped and the fog had finally disappeared, so Beniamino was able to enjoy his powerful car. He didn't give a damn about speed-traps: he had had an electronic device installed on the dashboard, giving him advance warning when one was coming up.

'You're rich enough to keep Sylvie, and have her move in with you,' I said, after a long silence.

He looked at me from the corner of his eye. 'Further proof that you understand precisely nothing about women. Taken out of her environment, that woman would turn into somebody else, and in a couple of weeks she'd be walking out, slamming the door behind her.'

'She's over forty,' I pointed out. 'So I doubt if she'll be able to go on dancing in nightclubs much longer.'

My associate heaved a heavy sigh. 'You're a hopeless fucking case. With her physique, Sylvie will be dancing for at least another ten years. By which time yours truly will be just a memory.'

Back at La Cuccia, I bumped straight into Virna, but she managed to avoid saying hello to me. I walked over to the bar and asked Rudy for an Alligator. Nothing ever escaped Rudy.

'I'll fix it nice and strong,' he said, 'your girlfriend's in the vilest of moods this evening.'

I hung around for ten minutes or so, then slipped upstairs to Max's. I briefed him on the latest developments, then went next door to my own apartment to get some sleep.

Corradi was depressed. His voice was tired and hoarse. 'I'm in deep shit, Alligator. Without that statement from the Colombian, I've no hope.'

'It's not over yet. We have a promising lead on the mule's contact. It seems he's an Italian who traffics Colombian girls to Japan. It could even be somebody who knows you . . . somebody who maybe fed the police your name. Any ideas?'

Nazzareno was silent for just a second too long for me not to sense something was up. 'No,' he said at last, curtly, immediately clearing his throat.

I glanced at Max and Beniamino who were following the conversation on the speaker. Max scribbled something on a sheet of paper then flashed it in my direction. 'He's lying,' it read.

There was no doubt about it. 'You do know the guy, don't you?' I burst out. 'Look, Nazzareno, this isn't the moment to jerk us around. We've absolutely got to know who it is.'

There was a further moment's silence, then Corradi hung up.

'Shit,' I shouted. 'What the fuck has got into that dickhead? Does he really want to croak in prison?'

Rossini smoothed his moustache. 'Let's forget about Corradi for now. He's upset and we'll never force him to talk. Let's work instead on the Colombian scene, see what the girls can give us. Sooner or later, we're sure to come up with something.'

The same girl who had given us the information about La Tía now recommended we get in touch with a former hostess, a Colombian woman who had arrived in Italy about twenty years earlier, at a time when Colombian girls were still something of a rarity. She had worked in every nightclub in the area and then, when competition from younger compatriots had forced her out of the scene, she had turned to prostitution, working from home on an appointments-only basis. Later she had got to know an Italian who decided to exploit her business acumen by opening a brothel. It was nothing special, just five rooms at the back of a Latino-style bar on the coast at Lignano Pineta.

The joint was called Puerta del Sol. When we arrived it was heaving. There was a salsa-group playing, and people were dancing close to the tables. We perched on a couple of barstools and in the space of two minutes had identified the working girls. They were all young, all from Eastern Europe, all blonde, and all had faces etched with disappointment. Italy wasn't such a paradise after all. The barman approached and asked us what we wanted to drink.

'Go and get the landlady,' Rossini ordered.

He looked us up and down for a second or two, then decided it was advisable to obey.

Her real name was Luisa Villazimas Serrando, but everyone called her Luisita. A couple of minutes passed and then she made her entrance. Slim and well-dressed, she displayed the arrogant and detached attitude of someone who has carved out a career for themselves and doesn't want any trouble. Her nostrils were reddish at their base. It looked like the lady had a habit.

She folded her arms. 'What do you want?'

'A quiet place to talk,' I replied.

'We can talk just fine right here.'

'No, we can't,' Rossini retorted. 'It's either your office or one of the backrooms where you get the blonde chicks to screw for you.'

Luisita stiffened. Then she parted her lips just wide enough to show a row of yellowed teeth. It was her way of letting us know we weren't fazing her. 'Leave now, or I'll have the bouncers toss you out.'

Beniamino threw his cigarette butt on the floor without bothering to stub it out first and then gave the lady one of his classic pieces of advice. 'I saw them on the way in, that pair of jerk-offs. Go ahead and call them. First I'll cripple them with a bullet through the knee, then I'll come back with a jerrycan of petrol and burn this joint of yours to the ground.'

Luisita looked him in the eye, while deciding what to do. Clearly she didn't like what she saw. 'This way,' she said.

She led us to a small windowless office and sat herself down on the only chair. 'I'm listening.'

Beniamino glanced at the desk, littered with bills, then sat on its edge. 'We're looking for an Italian who exports Colombian prostitutes to Japan.'

Luisita took her time about answering, which was a mistake. 'Why come and ask me about it?'

'Because you're the oldest Colombian hooker in the business,' Rossini replied.

'Besides, there's just no way you know nothing about it,' I added.

'As it happens, you're both mistaken. I know nothing about it at all.'

Old Rossini picked up the phone receiver and hit her on the head with it, not very hard, just hard enough to make her understand the direction in which the conversation was heading. Then he bent down over her and whispered in her ear.

'No more bullshit. Otherwise I'll cut not only your face but those of your hookers, too. After that, I'll have the joint closed down. You'll end up turning tricks outside the army barracks for a living.'

The lady touched her head, assessing the damage. She must have taken quite a few beatings in her lifetime. 'I've got family in Colombia. If I talk, the prostitution rings back home will take revenge. I'd rather blow army grunts.'

Luisita had guts to burn. I decided to change tactics. 'We're seeking the individual in question for a reason that has nothing whatever to do with prostitution, and nobody will ever know it was you that gave us the tip-off.'

She lit a cigarette. Her hands were shaking. 'I have to know the truth. I need to know I can trust you.'

I looked at my associate, who nodded his assent. 'All right,' I said. 'It has to do with coke, a Colombian drug mule killed in prison, and an Italian who was arrested instead of the man whose name we're seeking. That's all I can tell you.'

Luisita finished her cigarette. 'The man you're looking for is from Venice. His name's Bruno Celegato. He used to work as a sailor, when he was younger. He's always been involved in trafficking. When he was working the boats, he got to know gangsters from all over the world, but somehow he never became a boss himself.'

'So where can we find him?'

'The last time I saw him was at least three years ago. He was living in Mestre.'

I touched her lightly on the shoulder. 'You have nothing to worry about.'

On our way out, I took a look at the bouncers. It was a good thing Luisita had fallen for Beniamino's bullshit threats. They were big guys with boxers' broken noses: they would have beaten us up with professionalism and spite. I would have folded at the first blow. Rossini would have defended himself, playing dirty the way he had learned on the streets of Milan, using stools and bottles as weapons. But he would have ended up on the carpet just the same. Later he would have exacted revenge and the two goons would have paid a heavy price for their handiwork. One time, a Turkish bouncer, after a dispute in a swish nightclub near Varese, had surprised him with a straight jab to the chin. The Turk was using a knuckleduster and Rossini passed out even before he hit the deep-pile carpet. A couple of weeks later, he waited for the guy outside his house, and shot him through the left elbow with a .357 magnum.

Out on the street, I took my associate by the arm. 'Was it really necessary to hit her with that phone?'

'Yes, it was. I didn't enjoy it, but it had to be done.'

'I don't agree.'

Rossini flew into a rage. 'You're just a fucking amateur. Don't bust my balls with this crap of yours. That lady makes her living off the back of young girls. Do you really imagine she doesn't raise her hand to them when they don't feel like going to one of the backrooms to get fucked by some yokel?'

I raised my hands in surrender. 'All right, all right. Let's go after Celegato.'

Rossini took his cell phone from the pocket of his overcoat. 'I'm phoning Mansutti. Tomorrow, we're going to have to have a little word with Nazzareno.'

The following morning, the three of us met in Max's kitchen for breakfast. Rossini was still smarting from our altercation the day before. Max took his side.

'Under the circumstances, it was necessary, Marco. That's all there is to it. Physical violence, blackmail and money are the springs that make people want to talk. They're the only available tools and we have no option but to use them. Without them, none of our cases would ever get solved.'

I decided to let it go, and changed the subject. 'Bonotto's expecting us. You ought to come too, Max. It's time we took some important decisions.'

On our arrival, the secretary told us we would have to wait. Bonotto was busy with another client. We gave her our cell phones, made ourselves comfortable in the waiting-room, and began flicking through the usual heap of magazines. I settled down with an automobiles monthly. Apparently Skoda was about to launch its latest model. I decided I would go and take a look at it once I had finished the case and received my fees. I had done over 200,000 kilometers in my old one. It was time to trade it in.

Avvocato Bonotto accompanied his client to the door, then

came over to greet us. He told his secretary to phone the bar and have four coffees sent up. From behind his desk, he surveyed us thoughtfully. 'Something important must have come up, if all three of you are here.'

I picked up his chunky desk-top lighter and lit a cigarette.

'We've discovered the identity of the late Arías Cuevas' Italian contact. His name is Bruno Celegato and, according to information dating back three years, he lives in Mestre.'

The lawyer's eyes fell open with surprise. 'Celegato. He used to be a client of mine. I defended both him and Corradi when they were tried for the murder of those two police officers. As far as I know, he is—or was—Corradi's best friend.'

Max, Rossini and I glanced at one another. We couldn't tell Bonotto about our direct line to his client, but we now possessed an explanation for the way Nazzareno had behaved on the phone the previous day.

'That explains,' said Rossini, thinking aloud, 'how the cop, Nunziante, found out that Corradi killed the two patrolmen in Caorle.'

The coffees were brought in, giving us some time to arrange our thoughts.

'How are you thinking of proceeding?' the lawyer asked.

'Well, given the involvement of the law enforcement agencies, with the greatest possible circumspection,' Max replied.

'For the time being, we can reasonably assume Celegato struck a deal with the police and Finanza to frame Corradi. But before we make any kind of move, let alone anything involving the courts, we're going to have to clarify every single aspect of this case. And that is going to entail some careful investigative work.'

'We don't have a lot of time,' Bonotto objected, sounding worried.

Beniamino opened a packet of cigarettes and looked the lawyer in the eye. 'The quickest way would be to drop in on

Celegato and ask him to tell us what's going on. I'm sure he'd cooperate, but if he's in that tight with the cops, we could end up in trouble ourselves, at which point there would be nothing more anybody could do for your client. You're going to have to be patient, Avvocato.'

'Go and talk to Nazzareno,' I urged the lawyer. 'Get him to tell you every last detail that might possibly be of help to us. Talk to the investigating magistrate too, and see what you can find out.'

'Okay.' Bonotto buzzed his secretary and asked her to bring in the file relating to the trial for the jeweler's shop robbery in Caorle and the killing of the two patrolmen.

He flicked through it and then handed me a newspaper cutting with a photo of the two accused men. 'Unfortunately I can't help with Celegato's present whereabouts. At the time of the trial, he was still living in Venice at his mother's place.' I shook his hand. 'Don't worry. Finding him is the least of our problems.'

After lunch, as we savoured our liqueurs, we discussed the best way to handle Corradi. I had wanted to broach the subject earlier, but Old Rossini hadn't wanted to spoil his enjoyment of the pastissada de cavàl that Max had prepared for us, or indeed the bottle of Amarone that he had decanted an hour earlier, treating it as if it were holy water.

'I don't wish to talk about piece-of-shit snitches while I'm eating delicacies,' Rossini had stated, leaving no room for argument.

As the Calvados, vodka and grappa came round for the second time, I glanced at my watch. 'Our telephone appointment is in ten minutes,' I said.

The time galloped past, and when I dialled the number I just had to hope everything would go okay.

'Ciao, Alligator,' Corradi said, sounding like a zombie.

I dispensed with greetings. 'Your best friend. Bruno Celegato. It's thanks to him you're in prison. And you also have him to thank for tipping Nunziante off about the two patrolmen. What are you going to do?'

'I don't know. I still can't believe it.'

'I can understand that it came as a blow, but we really need something we can work with. I mean, if we could just find out the terms of the deal Celegato has struck with the cops, maybe we could find a way of getting you out of prison.'

'I know nothing whatsoever about it. I had no idea he was trafficking coke.'

'What about his trips to Japan?'

'Sure, he always talked about that. It was Bruno who first got me interested in Colombian women.'

'There's really nothing more you know?'

'I give you my word. After the Caorle job, we decided to quit working together. All I knew was what he kept telling me up until just a few days before I was arrested, which is that he was involved in nothing but prostitution.'

'Do you at least know where he lives?'

'Yeah. Mestre, Via Tevere twenty-one, third floor.'

'What car does he drive?'

'A yellow Saab convertible.'

'Don't go blurting this all out to Victoria. Nobody must know we've identified him.'

'I have no desire to talk about this to anyone.'

I hung up. 'So there we have it. We don't know a fucking thing.'

Max put the lid back on the pastissada. 'There's nothing for it. We'll have to tail him.'

'Shit,' I said. 'That's the part of this job I hate the most. It's time-consuming, boring as hell, and utterly unpredictable.'

Rossini pulled on his overcoat. I did the same. There was no point complaining.

*

Via Tevere was a side-turning off Via Cà Rossa, a long road that snaked its way through Mestre and then out to a district known as Favaro Veneto. It wasn't the best place for a stake-out. Both the police and the Carabinieri had barracks in the neighbourhood and the streets were patrolled constantly. We had parked my Skoda about fifty meters from the block of flats where Celegato lived, in a spot that gave us a good view of his car.

As the third squad car went past, Rossini erupted in irritation. 'Look, Marco, we can't stop here. In half an hour at most, they'll be asking us for our ID.'

'You're right. What we need is a van.'

Rossini knew just where to look. There was a friend of his back in Punta Sabbioni who, despite his clean criminal record, had a weakness that he needed at all costs to keep from his wife. And, as it happened, he owed Rossini a lot of favors.

Three quarters of an hour later we drove into Punta Sabbioni. Rossini told me where to drop him and asked me to wait in the car-park of a restaurant he pointed out to me. When I saw him pull up in a little Japanese van, I knew the whole stakeout was going to be utter torture. There was a sign on the side that read: 'Pescheria Irma. Fresh and deep-frozen fish and seafood.'

I lowered the car window. 'You can take that right back where you found it. I've absolutely no intention of stinking like a mullet for the rest of my days.'

Beniamino wagged his index-finger at me. 'You've made up your mind to piss me off, right? I've put my entire business on hold for this crappy investigation of yours and you have the nerve to play the fine-nosed fop?'

'There's no way we can stay shut up in that thing for hours on end.'

He flashed a deadly smile at me. 'Yeah? Go tell that to Corradi.'

I got out of the car and into the van. The stench was intense even in the driver's cabin. But when we got to Mestre and parked outside Celegato's place, and there was no choice but to hide in the back, it was like being pitched into the hold of a fishing-boat. Rossini never batted an eyelid. I took out a cigarette and stuck it in my mouth. Absent-mindedly, Rossini pulled it back out and threw it on the floor. 'No smoking in here,' he said, 'these goods are perishable.'

'Tell me you're joking.'

'Not at all. Right now I quite fancy a cigarette too, but we can't. The owner of the van would notice and that would mean bye-bye van.'

I looked at him as if he were raving. 'Do I take it you're intending to use this trashcan for other stakeouts?'

'Sure. The fishing trade is a great cover here in Mestre.'

By the time Celegato decided to go out, it was almost ten o'clock. He looked nothing like the photo Bonotto had handed us but closely fitted the description that the Colombian had given the police. We slipped out of the back of the fish-van and climbed into the cab. Celegato got into his Saab convertible and headed for the centre of town. There he stopped, went into a bar and played billiards till around midnight. He then came out, got back into his car and drove to the train station. After circling a couple of times, observing the hookers, he stopped to talk to a blonde in her early twenties, probably an Albanian. They haggled over the price and the exact nature of the services, then the woman got in and they drove to a nearby hotel and went inside. A little later he drove home.

'We'd better hope this was one of his duller days,' I commented.

Rossini fidgeted with his bracelets. 'Given the number of cops in this neighbourhood, we can only really stake out his flat after about four in the afternoon, once it starts getting dark. And unless we get lucky, this isn't going to get us any-where anyway.'

The second day, Celegato left home a little after six in the evening. He took the main road for Treviso, floored the accel-erator, and in a matter of seconds had vanished.

The third evening, when he got into his yellow Saab, we switched to Rossini's car which we had parked nearby. We didn't want to lose all trace of Celegato two evenings running. He led us to the same bar and the same hotel as the first evening, though this time the girl had jet-black hair.

The fourth evening, he took the autostrada and headed towards Milan. He exited at Padova West and drove to a little village close to the city's industrial estate. Then, indicating as he turned, he swung sharp right into the car-park of a private swingers' club.

'This guy's got nothing but sex on the mind,' I snapped. Rossini made himself comfortable, tilting his seat back a little. 'Well, isn't he the lucky one! Sylvie's starting to suspect I have a lover.'

To our surprise, Celegato left the club a mere twenty min-utes later. 'That's odd,' Rossini commented. 'As an unaccom-panied man, it costs you three hundred and fifty thousand lire to get into this joint.'

We followed Celegato back to Mestre where he picked up the same blonde girl as on the first evening. I gave my associate a nudge. 'It looks like he didn't go to that club for sex after all.'

'Right. Starting from tomorrow, we can wait for him there. I'm positive he'll show up.'

I smiled with satisfaction. Not so much because we were finally making some headway with our investigations, more because we could at last jettison the stinking fish van. I was sick of going home every night and stuffing all my clothes into a plastic bag to drop off at the cleaners the following morning.

At La Cuccia, I found Max and Victoria sitting at my table,

chatting. Virna intercepted me as I made my way over to join them. 'She's been waiting for you for a while. She must have something really major to tell you.'

'Just bring me a drink, please. And don't make yourself ridiculous.'

Max handed me the chair and clapped me on the shoulder by way of greeting. Victoria stood up and shook my hand. She was wearing a long knitted dress, low-slung shoes with buckles, and her hair was gathered in a thick plait. As always, she looked absolutely beautiful. She turned to me with a sad, shy smile. 'I just dropped by to see if there was any news.'

'No, none yet, I'm afraid.' Glancing up, I caught Virna's stare and so hurried to add, in a diplomatic tone of voice,

'Don't trouble yourself to come by, Victoria. The minute we find anything out, we'll let you know.'

She leaned her head to one side and tugged at a ringlet that had escaped from her plait and was lying against her neck. 'I was hoping you had found out something about that man who takes girls to Japan.'

I decided to close the subject. 'It turned out to be a false lead. Nobody knows anything about it.'

Victoria stood up, calmly pulled on her leather coat, and did up the buttons. Another doleful smile and then she left.

Max poured himself some beer. 'Corradi's nights must be hell, lying there and thinking about her.'

I glanced at Virna, who had taken good care not to bring me the drink I had ordered. 'I hope Victoria will stay away from now on. My girlfriend doesn't like having her around.'

'I've noticed that. All the same, I wouldn't bank on Victoria staying away. She confided in me that she can't bear being all alone in that big empty house. It gives her the jitters. So in the evenings she does the rounds of the nightclubs, looking for someone who can sympathize with her situation . . . She'll be back.'

'All we need is a prison widow on the edge of a nervous breakdown. Listen, Max, I think we're onto something. I'll just get myself a drink and then I'll tell you all about it.'

After Max had heard me out, he took a long gulp of beer.

'I reckon you're right to keep an eye on the swingers' club. Celegato is acting really strangely. Have you ever been in a swingers' club?'

'No, I haven't, but Beniamino told me he has a few times. Apparently there are lots of small, low-lit rooms full of people having sex, any way the mood takes them. Mainly it's couples. The way it works is that entrance tickets for couples are relatively cheap, about a hundred and fifty thousand lire, whereas men who turn up on their own, like Celegato, have to part with three hundred and fifty thousand each.'

'It would be a perfect venue for a rendezvous.'

'Or to take delivery of a consignment of coke.'

'Right. But we must also keep an eye on the bar and the hotel where he takes the hookers. He goes there too often . . .'

'I'll call Rossini tomorrow and suggest he take a closer look. After all, the swingers' club doesn't open till nine in the evening.'

The next day, Rossini turned up just in time for dinner. Max wasn't in the mood to cook so we had to make do with a simple plate of pasta.

I grated some Parmesan over my tortiglioni. 'Did you manage to get that information I asked you about this morning?'

'Yes, I did,' Rossini said. 'I dropped in on Toni Vassallo. Do you remember him? When we were in prison in Padova, he was in cell twenty-six.'

I stopped chewing. 'Of course I remember him. He's the guy who got shot in the back by some jeweler and ended up in a wheelchair.'

Rossini turned to Max. 'It was really bad luck,' he recounted.

'He had been out less than a month and his brother had come up with this job, a real cinch, just to put him back on his feet financially after four years inside. The problem was that the jeweler had a hidden handgun which they failed to discover before emptying out the safe. So there they are outside the store, jumping into the getaway car, when out runs the jeweler and fires three bullets into Toni's back.'

'So what did Toni tell you?' I asked. At times I found that Beniamino's tales of the underworld went on longer than strictly necessary.

'Nowadays he deals in coke and ecstasy. He's the brains of the organization and his wife does the deliveries. He knows everything there is to know about the drugs market in Mestre and confirmed that both the bar and the hotel used by Celegato are places where drugs are bought and sold. Lately, there has been a spate of arrests and Toni is convinced there's a well-placed snitch at work.'

Max opened the fridge, looking for something else to eat.

'What this means is that Celegato is working full-time for the police,' he remarked, grabbing a salami and a jar of baby artichokes in oil.

'Did Vassallo name Celegato specifically?' Max enquired.

'Yeah, among others. Obviously, I showed no interest. But he did mention that Celegato is a good purchaser, constantly on the lookout for a channel capable of supplying a kilo of coke at a time.'

Celegato didn't show up at the swingers' club outside Padova that evening or the next. It wasn't till the third evening that Rossini and I once again saw the yellow Saab convertible pulling into the car-park. We gave him a five-minute start, then followed him in. The club was members-only but it cost nothing to join. All you had to do was hand over some ID, which was diligently photocopied and then filed, the idea being to deter maniacs and serial killers. We had to shell out a huge sum of money to wriggle out of these bureaucratic obligations, on top of the 700,000 lire for our two entrance tickets.

We split up at the bar and began exploring the various rooms, all of which were semi-lit, comfortably furnished both with beds and with sofas for spectators, and stocked with a vast array of condoms. In the first room I walked into, there was a lady on all fours fellating her husband while a line of gentlemen took turns silently and discreetly to penetrate her from behind. In the second room, two couples were sharing a bed, while a largeish group of men and women looked on.

A hand gripped my arm. It was Rossini, motioning me to follow him. We went into a room where two women were fondling one another while their respective companions, both fully dressed in jacket and tie, whispered words of advice and encouragement. From a sofa, Bruno Celegato surveyed the sex-act with an absent-minded gaze. He was listening attentively to what the man sitting next to him, a guy in his mid-thirties with long hair gathered in a ponytail and a week's beard, was saying to him. My associate and I had seen enough. We left the club and hid in our car.

Celegato was the first to leave but we didn't follow him. It was the other guy we were interested in. He emerged about ten minutes later and climbed into a dark blue Renault Clio. He took the autostrada for Venice, followed the Mestre bypass all the way around, then headed for Trieste. Later he turned off for Udine and after a while pulled up outside a flashy condominium complex in a densely populated neighbourhood.

He vanished into the main entrance of the building and a couple of minutes later a light went on at a window on the first floor. It was a real stroke of luck to discover the precise location of his apartment so rapidly.

'He's a flatfoot,' Rossini declared.

'He certainly looks like one.'

'What shall we do?'

'Tomorrow morning we wait for him and when he goes out, we follow him. Then we double back here and take a look at his apartment.'

Old Rossini smoothed his moustache. 'It won't be easy. These condos have porters. Besides, the lock on his door may not be so easy to pick.'

'Okay. But we have to know who this guy is and what he's up to with Celegato. Celegato's contacts with the cops in Mestre should be more than sufficient if all he's doing is snitching. He only has to phone them or meet them in some dark alley. Where's the sense of them meeting up in a swingers' club in Padova and then one driving home to Mestre and the other to Udine? Something else is going on here. Maybe this guy isn't a cop.'

'He's a cop all right. I'm certain of it.' Rossini looked at the digital clock on the dash. 'We'd better get a move on. We've barely got time to get to my place, pick up the tools, and get back here.'

At seven-thirty in the morning, the road where the presumed cop lived was bustling with people opening shops, leaving for work or taking their children to school. We slipped into a bar just opposite the condo's main entrance. We ordered a lavish breakfast and hoped the guy was an early riser.

He didn't disappoint us. He walked out of the condo on the dot of nine. In one hand he was carrying a stiff leather suitcase, in the other a dark blue bag of the kind filling stations used to give away for free. He drove straight to the autostrada, but this time followed the signs for Trieste. He then took the Ronchi dei Legionari exit and we followed him all the way to the parking lot of a small airfield. Then we watched as he boarded a ten-seater air-taxi bound for Rome.

'What a nice man,' Rossini chuckled. 'He's leaving us all the time we need to check out his apartment at our leisure.'

'We'll go in tonight. That way we won't have to worry about the porters.'

We wandered from one bar to another, then from a restaurant to a cinema, till finally night fell. By eleven o'clock the streets were cold and deserted. It took Rossini all of thirty seconds to open the condo's main door. Our steps along the corridor were muffled by the carpeting and drowned by the sounds of voices and TV sets from other apartments.

Breaking into the apartment itself took rather longer. Rossini had brought with him a set of picklocks designed and constructed by one of the most sophisticated house-breakers in Rome. He pulled on a pair of latex gloves and set about his work with meticulous care. We didn't want the occupant to notice we had broken in. The apparently flimsy lock raised our suspicions—it almost seemed an invitation to burglary. Maybe the place was alarmed or there were some James Bond-type traps left lying around, or a hair on the top of the door, or a matchstick in the doorjamb that would give us away.

A tinny little sound told us the lock had yielded. Rossini slowly opened the door and shone a torch around the room to see if there was an alarm liable to go off and force us to make a hasty getaway. But he didn't see anything and nothing happened, so we went in and closed the door behind us.

We checked that all the shutters were down and then Beniamino switched on the light. We found ourselves standing in the middle of a spacious one-room apartment, complete with kitchenette. The decor was devoid of taste and the furniture consisted of a bed, a couple of drab chairs, a bedside cabinet and a wardrobe.

We studied every detail with the greatest of care. Conducting a thorough search without leaving any trace of your presence requires patience and skill. This was not, however, our first time and we knew what to do. I opened the wardrobe and began to check through trouser and jacket pockets. The cop—if he was a cop—was certainly the untidy sort. I turned out half-empty packets of cigarettes, lighters, cinema tickets, and scraps of paper with phone numbers that I carefully copied out. In the middle of a pile of blankets, I discovered a little wooden box containing oil and pull-throughs for cleaning a gun. The drawers contained shirts and underwear of average quality, the kind of clothes worn by people on a state salary. A drug dealer could afford much better.

Rossini had finished with the bathroom and was now struggling with the drawer of a bedside cabinet. It was a matter of going through the picklocks until one worked. The drawer turned out to contain some odds and ends and a handful of love letters from a woman called Carla who wrote from Mantova. The envelopes were all addressed to Maresciallo Stefano Giaroli at the headquarters of the Guardia di Finanza—the enforcement arm of the Ministry of Economics and Finance—in Rome. I checked the dates. The most recent was postmarked just ten days earlier. I handed it to Beniamino. 'This marshal reeks of some kind of special agency,' he remarked. 'There's something major going on.'

'Yeah. I wouldn't mind betting he's a member of GOA, the Gruppo Operativo Anti-Droga. They run by far the best anti-narcotics operations in Italy.'

The following morning I dropped in at Renato Bonotto's law firm. I asked him for some more money, explaining that the investigation was turning into a bottomless pit. He opened a drawer and pulled out the standard yellow envelope.

Bonotto jotted the sum down in his desk-diary. 'I imagine you've not come to see me just for the money.'

'You're right. Our investigations have been making some progress but we don't much like what we've been finding out.

We're now convinced that Celegato is a pawn in a much bigger game, involving men from the Guardia di Finanza headquarters in Rome. If we're right about this, Corradi was put behind bars so that his one-time buddy Celegato remained free to continue working undisturbed as a police informant. To complete the picture that's emerging, though, I need to know how your talk with the magistrate in charge of the investigation went.'

Bonotto had stared me straight in the eye throughout, carefully weighing each of my words. 'Well, the attitude of the state investigators is rather odd, Buratti. And I'm not just referring to that lazy-assed, Judge Pisano. Yesterday, at the Public Prosecutor's office, I ran into Nunziante and Captain Annetta from Finanza. I came away with the distinct impression that they don't really give a shit. Pardon the vulgarity. As far as they're concerned, the investigation is done and dusted. They haven't the slightest intention of sanctioning any further enquiries. Corradi is guilty because he was caught red-handed and Arías Cuevas has died, bequeathing nothing but a bunch of statements that do my client no favors at all. All the investigators are doing is kicking their heels until it's time for Corradi to be arraigned.'

I ran a hand through my hair. 'Do you realize we're getting mixed up in a special operation run from Rome by the combined forces of the state police and the Guardia di Finanza?'

'Yes, I do. And my professional advice to you is to drop your investigation the moment you see any real danger of breaking the law.'

I got up and made for the door.

'Right now I can't see what the hell a defense lawyer is supposed to do in a case of this kind,' Bonotto said bitterly.

'The law is nothing but a cover for the petty vendettas and back-stabbing of a collection of state spooks.'

I turned round. 'Listen, Avvocato. You are the one person

who can get Corradi out of prison. If things work out right, you'll end up with a freshly shuffled deck of cards in your hand. And then it'll be up to you to play the right ones. That's what lawyers are for.'

Max the Memory had a plan. He laid it before us after a lunch that was both elaborate and hard to digest.

I poured myself some more coffee and spiked it with an ample quantity of Calvados. 'I don't like it,' I protested. 'It's too dangerous. The cops used on special operations are the brightest and the best trained. Any attempt to stitch them up could land all three of us back behind bars.'

'Fine. Then we'd better just abandon Corradi to his fate,' Max fumed.

Rossini smoothed his moustache. He was fizzing with excitement. I was outnumbered yet again. 'Well, personally, I think it's an excellent plan,' he said, giggling like a ten-year old. 'It'll be a real pleasure to hammer some super-spooks.'

I shook my head in exasperation. 'You're mad, the pair of you.'

Max took my face between his hands. 'Marco, these bastards frame or clear people just as they see fit and to hell with the law. The same lousy bunch that fucked us all over, our entire generation.'

'So?'

He let go of my face. 'So, for once in our lives, we get even with them.'

Signora Gianna welcomed us with a smirk. 'So you've come back to see that pair of dykes again, have you?'

'It's really just an excuse to see you again, Bella Signora,' Rossini replied.

'Damned clown,' she muttered, by way of insult.

Aisa opened the door in her dressing gown and with a towel

around her head. She surveyed us blankly. 'Doña Rosa is having a bath.'

Beniamino barged past her. 'Then tell her to hurry up.'

La Tía kept us waiting for a good twenty minutes. She then appeared in a dressing gown, but her hair was dry and she was perfectly made-up.

She took a gulp of her favorite rum. 'What do you want?' I aimed the remote at the television and switched it off.

'To offer you a deal.'

She bent her head, sensing a trap. 'Involving coke?'

'Yes. The best Colombian coke you can get your hands on.'

She smiled, displaying her yellow teeth. 'So where's the catch?'

Beniamino went over to the minibar and began to rifle through its contents. 'Maybe you should sit down. It'll take a while to explain.'

I stood up to make room for her, and went over to lean against the window. 'We've identified Guillermo's Italian contact. It turns out he's a full-time police informant. He's looking for a channel that can supply him with a kilo of coke per consignment. We figured you could sell it to him.'

La Tía folded her arms. 'And what do I get out of it? Apart from an international arrest warrant?'

'A big pile of dollars—and no arrest warrant,' I reassured her. 'This guy clearly doesn't need the coke in order to arrest a mule or identify the source back in Colombia. We're pretty sure it's intended for use in a police operation here in Italy and we want to monitor its movement, see what route the merchandise follows.'

La Tía evaluated the proposal while she smoked her way through a cigarette. 'Too dangerous. It's not in my interest.'

Old Rossini nodded several times. Then he spoke in a tone of voice that I had only ever heard him use just before he killed someone. 'Oh, but it *is* in your interest, Tía. Take my word for it. If you think it over, you'll see it makes excellent business sense.'

Doña Rosa broke into laughter, to relieve the tension. She had registered the absolutely serious nature of the threat—and Alacrán was too far away to offer her any protection. 'Well, if he pays half up-front, the second half on delivery, and agrees to a premium price for the goods, then okay. It ought to make me more than enough to cover this trip to Italy.'

'We'll ensure that the handover is as risk-free as possible,' Rossini said. 'And you can certainly demand a premium. After all, the Italian state will pick up the tab, drawing on the secret slush funds they set aside for special operations of this kind.' Approaching La Tía, Rossini added, 'To make sure you feel no temptation to hold on to the money and forget about despatching the coke, you will remain here in Italy for the duration. Along with your sweetheart, naturally.'

'That's impossible. Our tourist visas expire in a couple of days. We'll have no choice but to leave.'

Rossini's tone hardened. 'Out of the question. You're staying where you are. We'll get you new visas. We know the right people.'

A grimace of disappointment appeared on her face.

'You were thinking to rip us off, right?' Rossini said, with a snigger.

Rosa Gonzales shrugged her shoulders.

'How long will you need to bring your mule over?' I asked.

'A week.'

Rossini cast his bait. He paid Toni Vassallo, the paralysed drug dealer, a second visit. As they chatted about one thing and another, Rossini casually mentioned he had recently heard that the sales rep for a major Bogotá drugs trafficker had arrived in Italy and was looking for customers. A couple of days later, Vassallo's wife turned up on Rossini's doorstep, asking if he happened to know how the coke rep could be contacted.

Rossini smoothed his moustache. 'It's out of your league.'

'We know that. But there's this guy, Bruno—Toni says he's already talked to you about him—who would be willing to pay good money for the information . . .'

'Is he also willing to pay to find out the source of this information?'

Vassallo's wife turned white. 'What are you talking about, Beniamino? You know Toni would never rat on you.'

'There's nothing I know for sure any longer. But if he does let slip a single word, I swear I'll kill him. And I'll kill you too. Out of pity. A widow's life is just too miserable.'

Vassallo's wife was speechless with terror. In the criminal underworld, it was common knowledge that Rossini had eliminated quite a number of local gunmen belonging to the Brenta Mafia. She got up to go, but Rossini caught her arm.

'It was only a warning. I just don't want to land in the shit on some drug-dealing rap. That's all. The Colombian woman is about fifty. Every two or three days, she has dinner at Ristorante Barchessa, by the river at Caposile.'

I was in the livingroom, eavesdropping on the conversation. I had been staying at Rossini's place for a couple of days, while we waited for just such a visit. As soon as Vassallo's wife was out of the house, Rossini came into the room, smiling from ear to ear. 'Celegato's walking straight into the trap,' he said.

Rossini then left for Treviso, saying he would be back at six that evening. He had to pick up the new visas for La Tía and Aisa. He had contacted a bent cop he knew in the city's passport office who had agreed to sort out the problem for a reasonable sum.

He arrived back earlier than expected and we set off for Jesolo to see La Tía. For once, Signora Gianna abstained from any comment, keeping her eyes fixed on the magazine she was thumbing through.

'I wouldn't mind betting she's had a run-in with La Tía,' I hazarded.

I had guessed right. The landlady had had the temerity to make an unfriendly remark to Aisa as she walked past her desk one day on her way out to buy cigarettes and rum. The minute Doña Rosa heard about it, she went straight downstairs and pressed her hairpin up against Signora Gianna's throat, murmuring a phrase in Spanish which the landlady had understood imperfectly, though its general drift was clear.

La Tía related this with gusto and took offence when Rossini reprimanded her. 'You're not in Bogotá. You can't afford to throw your weight around like that. Here, you're just another fucking third-world tourist with a forged visa. If the landlady reports you to the police, our plan is fucked.'

'Take it easy, hombre, take it easy. Nothing happened.'

Rossini tossed the two visas on the bed. 'Bullshit. Behave professionally and cut out the attitude crap.'

They stared each other out and I decided to intervene to

prevent an exchange of slaps and hairpin thrusts. 'Our man has swallowed the bait and will be showing up at the restaurant.'

La Tía glanced at me with contempt. 'When?'

'The day after tomorrow.'

'The goods will be here in three days. Have you thought about how to do the handover?'

'Yeah, we have. We'll use the overpass technique.'

'I know it well. In Colombia too it's all the rage.'

'The purchaser will want to try a sample.'

'Claro.' She got up and went over to the bedside cabinet, crossed herself and picked up the statuette of Our Lady of Lourdes, full of holy water. She unscrewed the Madonna's head and pulled on a thread attached to the stopper. Out came an aluminium tube that had once served to safeguard the aroma of an Apostolado cigar.

La Tía waved the tube under my nose. 'Our Lady of the narcos,' she said.

As soon as we were outside, Rossini did an impression of her. 'Our Lady of the narcos . . . I swear the next time she says that I'll give her a good slapping.'

I stopped in a tobacconist's doorway. 'Look, I don't like her either and, personally, I can't wait for her to go back home to Colombia. But could you try to avoid a head-on clash with her? She's accustomed to never backing down. There's a risk that one day she'll plant that goddamn hairpin in your heart.'

Beniamino chuckled. 'Not her. Aisa is the dangerous one. While I was busy rowing with La Tía, she took up position behind me, and prepared to strike. I spun around just to let her know that trick wouldn't work with me and, well, the look on her face was not a pleasant sight.'

Max's study had been turned into an operations center, complete with microphones, recording equipment, radio trans-mitters, infrared night-vision scanners and a digital videocamera. Max listened with evident satisfaction to our account of the latest developments.

I looked him in the eye. 'Celegato is sure to turn up for the first meeting with La Tía with the cops in tow. Then, when it comes to handing over the money and taking delivery of the coke, he'll come trailing the same gaggle of police and Guardia di Finanza. I can't understand why you aren't more concerned. I'm shitting myself.'

Max poured me out a large dose of Calvados. 'Everything's under control, Marco. We're really going to screw them.'

'I still don't share your optimism. This is the first time we've ever taken on the police directly, and we have no experience in this area. I'll tell you something else. When I first started doing this work, the only rule I gave myself was never to accept an investigation that clashed with official enquiries.'

'Have you got a better idea?'

'No, I haven't. But I don't like the direction this is heading in.'

'It's too late. Now we've started, there's no turning back.'

'That's exactly what I don't like about it.'

The choice of venue for the meeting between Celegato and Rosa Gonzales left little to chance. The restaurant was near the banks of the river Sile and the plan was for La Tía to both arrive and leave aboard a speedboat. We wanted to make sure the cops couldn't pursue her. The coke was already on its way and Doña Rosa was going to hint to Celegato that the goods were close to hand. We were going to follow the negotiations and record the conversation.

Old Rossini had got hold of a boat with a flat keel and a quiet but powerful motor enabling us, if necessary, to shake off any police or Finanza motorboats among the sandbanks of the lagoon. The owner, a professional smuggler, handed it over to us at Cortellazzo, and in under twenty minutes we had reached

Jesolo, where La Tía was waiting for us at a bend in the river, hidden by a dense clump of poplars. I helped her to clamber aboard and then handed her a black raincoat with a hood. Rossini and I were both wearing black coveralls and bala-clavas.

As we approached Caposile, I radioed ahead to Max, hidden among piles of crates and boxes at the back of a super-market, from where he was keeping a watch on the restaurant parking lot using a night-vision scanner.

'Any news?' I asked.

'At this moment our friend is sitting at the bar. The others are hiding in a van, a white Fiat Ducato with dark-tinted win-dows. Given the tangle of aerials on its roof, I should guess they're planning to follow the conversation using a directional microphone.'

I explained the situation to La Tía and reminded her what to do in case of danger. 'If the cell phone in your bag starts ringing, it means the cops are on their way into the restaurant. You just get up, go into the kitchens, slip out the back and run down to the edge of the river. Beniamino will cover you.'

Rosa Gonzales climbed out of the boat and walked towards the lights of the restaurant, about fifty meters away. Rossini picked up the stiff leather case he had brought along, extracted a Browning .300 Winchester Magnum and, using a small screwdriver, adjusted the focus on its infra-red telescope. It was a weapon designed for hunting wild elk, fitted with an enhanced ten-shot loader and bullets that weren't in the slight-est bit bothered by bullet-proof jackets or the kind of steel-plating used in police cars and motorboats.

Beniamino pointed the weapon at La Tía's back. 'If she doesn't run fast enough, the only bullet to reach its target will be hers.'

I took my binoculars from their case and observed the win-dows of the restaurant. 'That would be senseless murder,' I retorted, watching La Tía take her place at the table she had reserved.

'You surely don't imagine I'd open fire on the police just to save the hide of a narcotics trafficker?'

'Of course not. All you have to do is fire in the air to create a diversion. If they nab her, we simply leg it as fast as we can.'

'You really are a hopeless fucking case, Marco. If she got nabbed because I'd failed to kill the cops, you can be sure she'd get her own back by trading us for a reduced sentence.'

'I don't think she'd do that.'

'There are far too many uncertainties. Which is why the best thing is to make quite sure temptation doesn't come her way.'

Celegato walked into my field of vision. I watched him bend down towards Doña Rosa, who activated the microphone concealed in the lace collar of her blouse.

'My name's Roberto,' Celegato lied, in almost perfect Spanish.

'Do we know one another?'

'No. But we have some friends in common who can vouch for me.'

'And why should they need to?'

'Just to establish that I'm someone who can be trusted, and a good purchaser.'

Rosa Gonzales got up and stood behind Celegato. Pretending to kiss him on the neck, she quickly frisked him. 'You wouldn't happen to be wired, would you?'

'Check all you like. But I told you, I'm someone you can trust.'

La Tía returned to her seat, smiling like a newly-wed. They ordered dinner. The wine waiter opened a bottle for them. Celegato raised his glass. 'To business,' he said.

La Tía ignored him. 'You're going too fast for my liking. Who are these friends we're supposed to have in common?'

'Carlos Rimadas Ríos and Juan Lopez Pinero,' Celegato

replied, naming two of the most powerful prostitution bosses in Bogotá.

La Tía nodded, appearing impressed by the eminence of Celegato's references. In fact she was wondering how much Ríos and Pinero would be willing to pay for the information that Celegato was a police spy. Well, she would discover that once she got back to Colombia. 'Obviously, I'll have to see if that checks out,' she said. 'Do I recall you saying you were a serious buyer?'

Celegato got straight to the point. 'I need a kilo of at least eighty-five per cent pure cocaine.'

La Tía chuckled sarcastically. 'You said you were a serious buyer. A kilo is small-time. It's smuggling for paupers.'

Celegato attempted to regain lost ground. 'The first consignment is just to test the channel. After which, the amounts acquired would obviously increase substantially.'

'And how much would you want to pay?'

Celegato pitched a lowish figure, expecting to negotiate. La Tía chewed her food slowly, then named her price, exactly twice the going rate. 'Not a dollar less. Otherwise, fuck off out of here. I've no time to waste.'

Celegato was silent for a moment, clearly disconcerted by La Tía's resolute approach. He took a sip of his wine. 'With a price that high, delivery will have to be extremely rapid.'

La Tía ripped a mussel from its shell. 'The day after tomorrow. You give me fifty per cent now and the rest on delivery.'

'I haven't got the money on me. I didn't think we'd reach a deal so fast.'

'So what the fuck were you thinking? I get the feeling you're some kind of clown.'

Tired of her insults, Celegato changed his tone. 'You want to calm down. You're not in Colombia now, you know. We do business differently here. I can let you have the entire sum on delivery.'

Doña Rosa remained composed. 'The day after tomorrow at the Tre Scalini restaurant in Portogruaro.'

'Fine.'

'I imagine you'd like to test the quality of the goods, right?'

'Obviously.'

La Tía took a small silver box from her handbag. 'Go to the toilets and have yourself a good snort.'

As soon as Celegato had disappeared, La Tía got up and made her way quickly to the kitchens and then out the back of the building. Old Rossini kept his gun trained on her till he was quite sure no one was following her. I helped her to climb on board and then radioed Max. 'Everything went fine. We're out of here.'

La Tía's mule arrived the following day on a coach packed with pilgrims returning from Lourdes.

When Rossini and I walked into their hotel room, Aisa was busy extracting aluminium cigar tubes from statuettes of the Virgin Mary. Rosa Gonzales stashed five in the freezer compartment of the minibar and then emptied the contents of all the others into a plastic container. Aisa added crushed Naproxen Sodium tablets—normally used to treat headaches—until the quantity of coke La Tía had subtracted had been made up.

As soon as he saw what they were up to, Rossini burst out laughing. 'You're ripping him off. You promised him eighty-five per cent pure coke.'

Doña Rosa shrugged her shoulders. 'Yeah, well I need some samples for my new clients. Besides, he won't notice a thing. I've never met such an amateurish buyer.'

I lit a cigarette. The stench of the coke, resembling urine, was turning my stomach. 'If he hadn't had the cops on his back, Celegato wouldn't have been in such a hurry to reach an agreement, or so willing to bend over backwards. They're in one hell of a hurry to get their hands on the goods. I'm really curious to know what they'll use them for.'

Within a couple of minutes, Aisa's and Doña Rosa's expert fingers had packaged the drug in plastic sachets, each weighing approximately 100 grams, which they then hid in a box of dog biscuits.

I took the box and placed it under my arm. 'We'll take charge of the handover. And as soon as we can, we'll bring you your money.'

'Don't keep me waiting too long. I'm short of cash.'

Rossini smirked. 'Don't tell me you've already got through that roll you had stashed in the chair leg.'

La Tía shook her head in disappointment. 'Searching our room displays a real lack of respect.'

'We're truly sorry. We didn't realize we were dealing with such a sensitive flower.'

The waiter was going from table to table waving a cordless phone and asking the diners if there was a Signor Roberto present. Celegato raised his arm.

'Hola,' said La Tía.

'The other day, you just vanished.'

'Playing it safe, hombre, that's all.'

'And today you're late.'

'Actually, no, I'm not. I've decided we'll do the handover another way.'

'Why? You were the one who wanted the meeting here.'

'And now I want it someplace else. I never met you before and, for all I know, you could have turned up with the drug squad in tow.'

'I'm on my own,' Celegato snarled.

'So much the better. I left a package at the bar for you. You'll find it contains a radio-transmitter. Take the autostrada for Mestre and switch it on. Someone will get in touch, don't worry.'

Max and I were waiting in the toll plaza. As soon as we saw Celegato's yellow Saab flash past, closely followed by the cops' Fiat Ducato, we started tailing them, Max driving my Skoda while I took Beniamino's car.

Meanwhile, twenty kilometers away, Rossini was waiting on an overpass.

I called him on his cell phone. 'Celegato's on his way—and he's not alone.'

Then I took hold of the radio-transmitter tuned to the one Celegato had picked up at the restaurant.

'Roberto?'

'Yeah?'

'In a few minutes you'll come to overpass number thirty-nine. Pull onto the shoulder as soon as you've passed it, take the case containing the cash, get out of your car and await further instructions.'

Celegato did exactly what he had been told, while the Fiat Ducato continued for another 150 meters before pulling over and hiding in an unlit rest area. Max and I stopped our cars a short distance before the overpass and observed the scene through binoculars.

Celegato walked back along the hard shoulder looking up at the overpass, and stopped the moment he saw Rossini, wearing a balaclava and armed with a hunting rifle, suddenly appear at the railing above him. Using a length of cord, Rossini lowered the small ivory-colored bag containing the cocaine. Celegato took the bag, opened it, produced a switchblade, and pushed it into one of the sachets of coke. He tasted the drug with the tip of his tongue, running it over his gums. He then attached his briefcase to the cord. Rossini hauled up the case, checked its contents, and signaled to Celegato that he was free to go.

Max drove off to tail Celegato, while I stopped under the overpass to pick up Old Rossini. So far everything had worked like a dream.

Cars were passing at such speed that nobody could have gotten a clear picture of anything happening on the ground. The overpass trick was getting a bit old, but it was still pretty neat. You could monitor what was going on from above, and if anything went wrong you had a clear escape route. Ever since a series of morons with nothing to do on Saturday nights had taken to hurling rocks onto passing cars, the highways authority had numbered the overpasses. This had made things much easier, enabling us to tell the dealer precisely where to pull up. Max the Memory had come up with a good plan.

I didn't have to wait long before I saw Rossini squeezing through a gap in the wire netting he had cut an hour or so earlier. He chucked the rifle and the money on the back seat and removed his balaclava. 'Move over, I'll drive,' he said.

I was happy to let him take the wheel, and called Max. 'What's happening?'

'It's all under control. The van's doing about a hundred and ten kilometers an hour, so it's easy to follow. Take over from me in about ten kilometers . . . Hang on a sec . . . they're slowing down . . . Shit . . . they're turning off, taking the Cessalto exit.'

'You go straight ahead. We'll take it from here.'

When we reached the Cessalto toll plaza, we saw Celegato's Saab and the white police van parked just the other side of the toll booths. We didn't want to drive past them so, to gain time, Beniamino pretended he had mislaid his wallet and asked the drowsy tollbooth attendant to bear with him. We saw Stefano Giaroli, the Guardia di Finanza marshal whose flat we had searched, get out of the van, walk over to the Saab, and climb in alongside Celegato. They then got back onto the autostrada, travelling in the opposite direction, heading towards Udine. The van took off along a smaller road to Treviso. We quickly found our money, paid up, and tailed the Saab. We couldn't get too close, so I kept my eyes riveted on their tail lights, using a pair of twilight-factor luminosity Steiner binoculars that Max had lent me.

I asked Max to catch up with us. Another car might come in useful. When they left the autostrada at Udine, there was no longer any room for doubt as to their destination.

Rossini fiddled with his bracelets. 'They're heading for Giaroli's place for a little nap.'

I put the binoculars back in their stiff rubber case. 'This means we'll have to tail them tomorrow as well.'

'When Max gets here, we'll dump the rifle and the cash in the Skoda and park it right alongside the Carabinieri headquarters, just to be sure no car radio thieves get any bright ideas. Then the three of us can make ourselves comfortable under Giaroli's condo and wait till they take off again with the drugs.'

'What if they split up?'

'We follow whoever's got the coke.'

It was during Max's watch, at about six-thirty, that Celegato and Giaroli came out of the main door of the building. Celegato, carrying the canvas bag containing the coke, got into the Saab and moved off. Giaroli followed him in his dark-blue Clio. It was a freezing cold morning and the roads were covered in ice and jammed with cars and trucks. We succeeded in tailing Celegato and Giaroli without drawing attention to ourselves or ever completely losing sight of them.

From Udine they headed north, and after a few kilometers drove into the village of Tricesimo. For a moment, we had been worried they might be making for the Austrian border. Celegato pulled up outside the village primary school. Giaroli hung back, halting roughly fifty meters from the school, on the opposite side of the road. Max, Rossini and I had no choice but to follow developments from a considerable distance, through the powerful zoom lens on Max's videocamera. It was just before seven.

A woman arrived on a bicycle. She stopped next to the yellow Saab, took the canvas bag from Celegato and placed it in the basket on her handlebars, then calmly pushed her bike over to the school gate and unlocked it. Celegato's Saab then disappeared around a bend, followed by Giaroli in his Clio.

'They've gone. They must be using the school janitor as a courier,' Max remarked as he put the videocamera back in its case. 'Which means that, unlike us, they must already know exactly where the coke is headed. We're going to have to keep tracking it, I'm afraid.'

Old Rossini surveyed our surroundings. 'There's no way we can stay here. Tricesimo is just a village and we'd attract attention. And we certainly can't follow her in a car. We're going to have to use a bicycle.'

At that point I asked the wrong question. 'Which one of us is going to pedal his way through this freezing cold?'

My two associates turned towards me with an identical smirk.

'Why me? I haven't been on a bike since I was a kid.'

'You're the best athlete,' Beniamino joked. 'And the youngest,' Max added. Then they burst out laughing.

We drove through the village and on to Tarcento where I bought a mountain bike with every imaginable accessory. I rode it a couple of times around the square just to get used to the way it handled. We returned to Tricesimo with the bike in the trunk and, at midday, when the kids came out, I started cycling up and down.

A quarter of an hour later, the caretaker locked the school gate and got on her bike. I followed her, leaving a distance of about thirty meters between us. She stopped to buy some bread and then headed towards the outskirts of the village. Out of the corner of my eye, I noticed Giaroli's blue Clio parked up a side road. The woman's house couldn't be far off.

Twenty or thirty meters further on, the woman stopped at an old, tastefully renovated farmhouse surrounded by a large garden. A big, long-haired dog lolloped up to greet her, wagging its tail. She stroked and patted it as she closed the gate behind her.

I couldn't hang around there. Giaroli might see me from where he was parked. Searching for a place from which to keep an eye on the farmhouse I noticed a large abandoned villa a bit further up the hill. I rode up to it, leant the bike against the back wall and climbed in through a window. It was empty and clearly hadn't been lived in for a long time. I went upstairs and found a room that, using the binoculars Max had given me, provided a clear view over both the farmhouse and Giaroli's car.

I called Max, explained the situation, and we agreed to check in every half hour. The intense cold was becoming unbearable and I had to make frequent recourse to a bottle of Calvados that I'd had the foresight to bring along.

At two-thirty in the afternoon, a red Seat Córdoba pulled up at the farmhouse. A well-built though not particularly tall man got out of the car, unlocked the gate, and crossed the garden. The woman greeted him with a hug and then a kiss on the mouth. He took off his cap and responded with passion. For a fraction of a second, a Guardia di Finanza badge glinted in the sun. I refocused my binoculars on his uniform to discover his rank: he was a marshal. The dog nosed its way between the two lovers and the man patted it. I refocused on the dark-blue Clio. From a reflection inside Giaroli's car it was clear he was photographing the touching scene.

I swore through clenched teeth. Things were beginning to make sense. Mixed up in this whole mess, there was now this Guardia di Finanza marshal who at some point had started playing for the other team. This was going to make everything a whole lot more complicated, not just for us but for Corradi too: it was clear he was just an expendable pawn in a game where he didn't know the rules.

I was now looking at a cops-on-cops job. If we let ourselves get caught in the crossfire of a special operation involving police and Finanza, it could cost us our freedom, everything.

The only sensible thing to do was to beat an orderly retreat and leave Nazzareno to his fate. The trouble was that Beniamino and Max would never agree to that. And nor could I.

I took a long swig of Calvados and lit a cigarette. I was just so fucking terrified of going back to prison, and wondered what the hell I could do to stave off that fear. 'Stick it up your ass' I told myself angrily. I would never make it through another spell in prison but I had known that all along. The day I walked free, I swore I would never go back. But Corradi had never had anything to do with coke trafficking and there was no way he deserved to die in prison just to satisfy a cop's appetite for revenge. He had been tried and cleared for the killing of the two patrolmen in Caorle and that was that. The cops should stick to the rules. Apart from that, as an investigator, once you've taken on a case, you can't just walk away. Then there was Corradi's girl: Victoria didn't deserve to lose her man forever. I had no option. These were the cards I had been dealt and I would have to play them as best I could. To hell with the cops and magistrates.

Giaroli's Renault slowly reversed back down the side road. Once again, they obviously knew where the coke was headed from here. All they were doing at this stage was keeping an eye on the situation and gathering some trial evidence.

The man came back out of the farmhouse, wearing a tracksuit and a pair of sandals. He was carrying a bowl full of food which he put down for the dog. This was his home all right. I took a better look at the buildings. There were signs of recent and costly remodelling. Tuscan terracotta tiles had been used to repave the portico, and the steps had been resurfaced with Verona marble. On the salaries that a school janitor and a Finanza marshal earned, they could never have afforded such luxury.

I recontacted my colleagues and gave them a description of the marshal's car, promising to call them again the moment he made a move. I checked the Calvados bottle, counted my cigarettes, and hoped something would happen before too long.

The marshal stepped out of the house at four o'clock. He had swapped his sandals for a pair of trainers and was now wearing a brightly colored down jacket over his tracksuit. He placed the canvas bag in the trunk of the car and drove away, giving a neighbor a big, friendly wave as he sailed past.

The marshal was feeling confident. Nobody was going to pull him over and search his car. If he came to a roadblock, he would just flash his badge. Of course, had he known his colleagues were polishing a nice pair of made-to-measure handcuffs for him, he would have been less chirpy. But for now he had no reason to feel under any threat. He was committing the classic mistake all cops make when they turn to crime: they think they're untouchable, and so start making a whole series of blunders that in the end give them away.

Bent cops are tolerated by their peers, just as long as they don't get sloppy, and, above all, provided they never forget they're in uniform.

'He's moving. Heading for Udine,' I told Max.

'Okay. Slip out the back. We'll pick you up on the corner of the road that runs parallel.'

Rossini stopped the car just long enough for me to clamber aboard. 'Let's just hope we don't lose him,' he grumbled.

We caught up with the marshal's Seat a few kilometers further on, near the turning for Pagnacco. He was driving carefully, staying within the speed limit. After Udine, he followed the main road for Gorizia, turning off at San Giovanni al Natisone. As he passed a filling station, the cops' Fiat Ducato suddenly appeared out of nowhere and started following him. The marshal drove on until Corno di Rosazzo, a little village close to the Slovenian border, famous for its excellent wines. He continued through the village center and then swung through a gate and into the grounds of a small villa surrounded by vineyards. The van drove further up the hill before turning into the drive of a farmhouse.

Rossini smoothed his moustache. 'That's their monitoring base. This operation must have been going on a while. The marshal is in tight with a sizeable outfit, otherwise his colleagues would already have arrested him.'

Night fell very suddenly and we needed to get closer to the villa. I had an idea. 'We could try going through the vineyards.'

Max shook his head. 'The cops would pick us up with their infra-red binoculars.'

Rossini pointed to wood of beech trees just outside the cops' line of vision. 'From those trees we'll be able to keep an eye on the gate and the front door.'

We were forced to make a long detour through the fields but it was worth it. Old Rossini had calculated right. It was a safe position with an excellent view. We began to spy on the villa using our binoculars and videocamera. Two Alsatian dogs were roaming around the garden, without ever attempting to go out of the gate: this meant they were trained and dangerous. The landlord clearly didn't like intruders.

In the distance, we saw the headlights of a car approaching. A black BMW with Croatian plates pulled up alongside the marshal's red Seat. Three men got out. The front door of the villa opened and a man strode towards them, whistling at the dogs, calling them to heel. The four men greeted one another and remained in the light of the porch just long enough for us to get a good look at their faces.

'They look like old acquaintances,' Rossini commented.

'I recognize three of them,' I said. 'Apart from Bruno Celegato, I can make out Ennio Silvestrin and Alcide Boscaro. Veterans of the old Brenta Mafia. Even back then, they were involved in drugs. But I don't know who the other guy is, the one dressed like a ladies' man.'

Rossini cackled, apparently pretty pleased with himself.

'Gentlemen, let me present Vlatko Kupreskic, the Croatian chemist. He's freelance, works for whoever pays best. He has refined heroin for Russians, Chechens, Calabresi . . .'

The door closed and the men disappeared from view. I lowered my binoculars. 'What the fuck is a chemist doing in a coke trafficking ring?'

Max lit a cigarette. 'I'll tell you exactly what he's doing. What we're looking at is a drugs factory. In that villa they're manufacturing ecstasy, or rather super-ecstasy: sulphur, cocaine, amphetamine and caffeine. A bomb of a psycho-stimulant. And a kilo of coke is enough to make quite a few tabs of that stuff.'

'It's the latest thing,' Beniamino added, 'with a market price of fifty thousand lire a tab.'

Max pointed at the farmhouse where the cops were camped out. 'The way they're going about things, it looks to me like they're intending to blow the whole organization apart.'

'Fine,' I said sourly. 'The problem is, what the hell do we do now?'

We drove back to Udine and picked up my Skoda. Then we headed for Jesolo. Rossini and Max were in Rossini's car a couple of kilometers ahead of me. Max had his cell phone at the ready to contact me if there were any police roadblocks, but there weren't.

La Tía was happy to get her hands on the money. She and Aisa were getting ready to go out. 'You'll excuse us if we don't hang around but I have a meeting with a new client.'

A look of mock disappointment flitted across Rossini's face.

'Such a pity! We were really hoping to invite you two ladies to dinner and then take you dancing all night.'

Doña Rosa stared at him for a moment, then resumed applying foundation to her face and eyeshadow to her drooping lids.

Outside, I asked Rossini if he had been serious about invit-
ing Aisa and La Tía dancing.

'Certainly,' he replied. 'You could have danced the tango
with Aisa through until dawn. A real shame.' Then he chuckled
long and hard. At Punta Sabbioni, Rossini fetched the rifle
from my car and handed it over for safekeeping to a person he
trusted. Then he said goodbye to Max and me. 'I want to
spend this evening with Sylvie. I'll see you two tomorrow.'

'Drop by in the afternoon,' I suggested. 'Max and I will go
and have a chat with Bonotto tomorrow morning. And could
you call Mansutti and tell him we need to speak to Corradi
tomorrow afternoon?'

After a long, scalding hot shower and a quick dinner at
Max's, I went downstairs to the club. Rudy greeted me warmly
and passed on some amusing gossip while he fixed me an
Alligator. On the way to my usual table, I bumped into Virna.

'Well, well, well. I thought you'd gone for good. Possibly
with the dreamboat from your famous investigation,' she said,
looking away.

'Cut it out,' I snapped.

She started absentmindedly wiping the empty tray she was
carrying. 'Next week, I'm taking three days off work. I'm going
away with a friend of mine.'

'Girlfriend or boyfriend?' I asked, regretting the question at
once.

She turned towards me with a smile of contempt.

'Girlfriend.'

'And what about our weekend together?'

'Nothing doing, Marco. Right now I don't feel like spending
time with you.'

I sat at my table, had a drink, and swallowed my rage. After
a couple of minutes Max joined me. He ordered a Jamaican
beer. It was a good thing I had more pressing problems to solve.

'I'm planning to tell it to the lawyer straight,' I said.

'Bonotto needs to know what's happening. Maybe he can come up with some way of pulling us all out of this mess.'

'Fine.'

'And I want to clarify the situation with Corradi, too. He's our client, after all, and we need to know what he thinks.'

'Fine.'

I looked him straight in the eye. 'Bullshit, Max. You're not "fine" with it at all, are you?'

'You're mistaken. It makes absolute sense to explore every possible solution that doesn't require our direct involvement. But I'm afraid it may be a waste of effort. I'm convinced the only course realistically open to us is to engage the cops in direct negotiation. We know enough to blackmail them: either they set Corradi free and clear him of all charges or we screw up their special operation.'

I ran a hand through my hair. One time, while working on a previous case, Max, Rossini and I had ended up with the Brenta Mafia gunning for us and we had only escaped with our lives by blackmailing an investigating magistrate attached to the Venice anti-mafia unit. It was this same method that Max was proposing we use now. On the earlier occasion, we had threatened to screw up their investigation and it had worked. I reached my fingers down into my glass, took hold of the slice of apple soaked in Calvados and Drambuie and popped it into my mouth.

Max placed his hand affectionately on my arm. 'What's up with you, Marco?'

I decided to be straight with him. 'What we're up against here are supercops. As far as they're concerned, the law is nothing but a mass of hair-splitting technicalities that prevent them from putting criminals away. So they bend the rules whenever they get the chance—which is all the time. Sure, a negotiation might work. But these guys have long memories and they can fit us up any time they please. One morning you're getting into your car, the cops stop you and, what do you know, they find a kilo of heroin right under your seat. Or they take your name and plant it in the mouth of some supergrass. You know as well as I do how these people settle their scores.'

'We'll take care they can't identify us.'

'Use your head, Max. We've been rattling around northeast Italy questioning nightclub hostesses and bouncers and a bunch of other characters not famed for their discretion. "Taking care" isn't going to do it.'

Max gave me a sly smile. 'We'll find a way of covering our backs.'

'You've already got a plan, haven't you?'

Max got to his feet. 'Let's just say I have a couple of ideas. We'll talk them over tomorrow when Rossini gets here.'

I watched him as he made for the door, and when it closed behind him I just sat there staring at it blankly until I heard the voice of Eloisa Deriu launching into 'Non so se tu', a ballad by Bruno de Filippi, the grand old man of Italian jazz. Sitting at another table, my friend Maurizio Camardi took his soprano sax out of its case, assembled it with a few deft movements and stepped onto the stage to join the other musicians. I downed three Alligators, one after the other, after which I felt a great deal better.

Following my advice, Renato Bonotto had had an elegant little wicker basket installed on his secretary's desk where clients could leave their cell phones before entering his office for a consultation. He came out to greet us in person. 'I'm pleased to see you. I went to see Corradi yesterday and the attitude he is taking towards his trial . . .'

I raised a hand to interrupt him. 'Let's forget for a moment about Nazzareno's attitude. We've uncovered the back story of his arrest.'

Bonotto fell silent, keen to hear what we had to say. I glanced at Max. Reports were his job.

Max stretched his legs and rested his hands on his gut. 'We are now in a position to make a rough reconstruction of the entire sequence of events. On the twenty-sixth of December, Guillermo Arías Cuevas, a Colombian national, landed at Venice airport with a belly full of cocaine and was immediately stopped on suspicion. He admitted possession, decided to cooperate with the border police, and provided a physical description of his Italian contact. As the police report states, he removed one of his shoes "without any prompting," and handed the agents a piece of paper bearing the address of the Pensione Zodiaco, a small hotel in Jesolo, where he was supposed to meet the purchaser that afternoon. The police and the Guardia di Finanza quickly set a trap and Bruno Celegato fell right in. On reaching the police station in Jesolo and realizing he was facing a long spell in prison, Celegato, in his turn—fol-

lowing, as it were, the mood of the moment—decided to cooperate with the police investigation. He confessed to belonging
to an organization involved in the manufacture and distribution of super-ecstasy. He mentioned that, as well as some former members of the Brenta Mafia, the said organization
included a Finanza marshal. It's this snippet of information
that must really have given the police something to think
about . . .'

'I can just imagine,' said Bonotto. 'The chance arrest of a
Colombian drugs mule throwing open a hugely important line
of enquiry. At that point they would have made a couple of
quick phone calls to get authorization to set up a special operation.'

'While making quite sure they weren't going to get tied up
in red tape,' Max added. 'Their first move was to make
Celegato an inside agent so they could follow the movements
of the criminal organization and figure out its command structure and personnel. But things weren't that straightforward.
The Colombian had been arrested and the investigating magistrate was waiting to hear the outcome of the stakeout at the
Pensione Zodiaco. Also, by this time, there were a lot of police
and Guardia di Finanza officers in the loop. It was at this point
that Celegato himself suggested Corradi be arrested instead of
him. The decision to betray his best friend was no accident.
Nunziante, the station officer interrogating Celegato, had
sworn years previously to take revenge on Corradi for the
killing of two patrolmen during a botched raid on a jeweler's
shop in Caorle. Your client, as you will recall, was accused,
tried and eventually acquitted owing to a shortage of hard evidence. Celegato, however, knew for certain it was Corradi who
fired the shots, because Celegato was also involved in the
Caorle job. So Celegato serves up Corradi's head on a silver
platter, providing Nunziante with a couple of details that never
emerged during the enquiry into the deaths of the patrolmen,

and that pin down Corradi as the killer. Of course Corradi can't at this point be retried for the Caorle killings but, if they let him take the fall for Celegato, he'll be inside long enough for it to make no difference. So the police and the Guardia di Finanza go to the Pensione Zodiaco a second time, take up position along with the mule in the hotel room, and draw Nazzareno into the trap with a phone call informing him that Victoria, his woman, has been taken ill. As soon as the mule sees Corradi, he yells at him to make a run for it—just as an accomplice would—and this lands Corradi straight in jail.'

'They were lucky Victoria couldn't be reached on her cell phone,' the lawyer remarked.

'That's true. But, even if she had been, they'd have made another attempt at a later date. The decision to frame Corradi had been taken. It was just a matter of time.'

'So who killed the Colombian?' Bonotto enquired.

'Killers from his own syndicate. They were afraid he would talk,' I replied concisely. It was better if Bonotto remained unaware of the role La Tía had played.

Bonotto selected a sweet from a silver bowl on his desk and unwrapped it slowly. 'Can you produce evidence to document the existence of the super-ecstasy outfit and the special operation?'

'Yes,' replied Max, who then brought Bonotto up to speed with our latest investigations.

Bonotto sucked thoughtfully on his mint. When he finally spoke, it was with great bitterness. 'Given what we now know, I could put Celegato and the police officers on the witness stand at the preliminary hearing and make mincemeat out of the lot of them. If it weren't for the fact—and it's this I wanted to discuss with you when you arrived just now—that Corradi doesn't want to involve Bruno Celegato in the trial. He made it crystal clear to me yesterday that he's not interested in getting out of prison by pointing the finger at someone else. Even if that someone else used to be his best friend and has betrayed him in the vilest possible way. He has instructed me to defend him using nothing but the evidence that emerged during the police investigation.'

There was a long silence. Bonotto called his secretary and ordered the usual coffees. 'My client's attitude to the trial is nothing short of suicidal,' he resumed. 'And, quite frankly, I don't understand it.'

I poured a full sachet of sugar into my coffee. 'Corradi is almost sixty. The fact is, he has lived his entire life according to a particular rulebook . . .'

'I'm well aware that my client is a man of his time, but I'd like you to appreciate my position. I can't see how I can defend a client to the best of my ability—as my professional ethic obliges me—without availing myself of evidence that could acquit him.'

'Fine. But what do you want us to do?' Max asked.

'Try to talk him round. I've got an appointment with Victoria tomorrow. Maybe she can make him see sense.'

'Does Victoria know about Celegato's part in all of this?' I asked.

'No, not yet. Corradi hasn't yet told her anything.'

'Then cancel that appointment, Avvocato. I know enough old crooks like Nazzareno to be sure of one thing: their code of conduct doesn't allow for the women they love to interfere in decisions of this kind.'

'Marco is right,' Max said. 'She'd only make matters worse. We'll find a way of broaching the subject with him. But we can't promise anything.'

'All right,' Bonotto said reluctantly.

As we were leaving his office, Bonotto asked us pointblank, 'In Corradi's shoes, what would you two do?'

I looked at Max, who just shrugged. 'The same as him . . . I think,' he said.

*

Beniamino arrived at Max's apartment earlier than expected and in a foul mood. He grunted out a greeting, took off his coat and threw himself on the couch. 'We've got a problem. A big problem.'

I thought I would try guessing. 'Mansutti?'

'You got it. Our prison corporal is scared shitless. I called him yesterday evening and to begin with he absolutely refused to set up any more phone conversations with Corradi. In the end I managed to calm him down and got him to explain what the fuck was going on. It seems that a team from Prisons Intelligence has gone into Santa Maria Maggiore. They're investigating the killing of the Colombian and generally poking their noses in everywhere. Today's phone call to Corradi will be our last.'

Modelled on the US experience, Prisons Intelligence teams were a recent innovation in Italy. They operated inside prisons, spying on the activities of Mafia leaders and other gangsters held at the state's pleasure. In Italy, however, the Prisons Administration Department had had the bright idea of making it the prime objective of the units to nurture a new generation of grasses and supergrasses, especially among those belonging to foreign-based criminal organizations. For several years now, the legal profession and many of the country's politicians had been demanding the disbandment of the units, claiming they were responsible for a series of outbreaks of violence that had created grave tensions among prison inmates, and above all alleging that they habitually recorded conversations between prisoners awaiting trial and their lawyers.

Max filled the pasta pan with water and placed it on the stove. 'Do you reckon Mansutti will stand up to questioning?' For an aperitif, Old Rossini poured himself two fingers of wheat vodka. 'I doubt it. And if he blabs, Marco and I are fucked. We're going to have to eliminate him.'

I looked at him without saying a word. There was no need to.

'Come on, Marco, don't jerk me around. You know as well as I do what this guy is like. He's only on the take because otherwise he couldn't pay for his hookers. The man's got no balls.'

I looked to Max for his opinion. 'The murder of a corporal in the prison police wouldn't pass unobserved. The Prisons Intelligence unit would be sure to refocus their investigations on Mansutti and it's just possible someone saw you together.'

'Who said anything about murder?' Beniamino retorted. 'I was thinking more in terms of a road accident. Preferably tonight. He goes to the nightclub, fools around with his Thai chick and then, on his way home, drives into a tree or ends up in a ditch.'

'I see you've got it all worked out,' I scowled.

The old gangster got up and came towards me. 'Certainly,' he said. 'And I'll tell you something else, Marco. I'm happy to kill Mansutti. He's the kind of bent cop you just can't trust. You remember the time I had to slap him around? Well, I read in his eyes that night that if I ever ended up in prison, he'd see I paid. I put my money on the wrong horse. End of story.'

I nodded. Corrupt prison officers like Mansutti could be two-edged swords. 'When's the accident? Tonight?'

'Yeah.'

'Do you want me to come with you?' I asked.

'No. I'll take care of it on my own. Mansutti was my mistake.'

We ate in silence, watching the news on TV. Then it was time to phone Corradi. I turned on the speakerphone.

'This is going to be our last chat, Nazzareno. It's no longer safe.'

'Do you have any news?'

'Celegato is not just any old police informant. He has infil-

142 · MASSIMO CARLOTTO

trated a major criminal organization and the reason he ratted on you was so he could do his job better. We've gathered enough evidence for you to leave the preliminary hearing a free man.'

'Would I have to put others inside?'

'Yes. Celegato, some dope peddlers, and the cops that fitted you up.'

'Then nothing doing.'

'You're the client.'

'What would you do, Alligator?'

I decided to lie. 'I'd fuck Celegato and enjoy the rest of my life.'

'I can't do that.'

'The alternative is prison.'

'I'm not going to stoop to his level.'

Beniamino decided to intervene. 'This is Rossini.'

'I've heard of you.'

'My answer to your question is as follows. I'd blow up the cops' special operation and then see how the pieces fall to earth. They can't just use you as a kleenex. You're a man.'

'That's exactly the way I see it.'

'Are you sure?'

'Absolutely.'

'What about your friend Bruno? If you ask me to, I'll take care of him.'

'No. That's my problem. If I get the opportunity to settle that score, I'll take it. But these are not matters I can delegate to others. Alligator?'

'Yeah, I'm here.'

'If things go badly, I want to be sure Victoria is looked after. Will you help me?'

'Sure. That I can do for you free of charge.'

I hung up, removed the card from the cell phone and chucked it in the bin. It was best to be rid of it. It was no use any more and once Mansutti was dead, the cops might fancy taking a look at the call records.

'It seems Max has a plan for putting the skids under the special operation,' I told Rossini. The old gangster just grinned and made himself comfortable on the couch.

Corporal Vincenzo Mansutti was a worried man. As part of their investigation into the killing of the Colombian prisoner, the men from the Prisons Intelligence unit were attempting to discover the identity of the prison officer who had reported to Bonotto the sequence of events surrounding the murder, thereby giving the lawyer the leverage to oblige the prison governor to redirect the murder enquiry. They suspected that the culprit was a low-ranking officer who had probably been attached to the Venice prison for some time and also that he had done it not for the love of justice but for money. The list that the unit had compiled comprised fifteen names, including Mansutti's. He wondered whether, under the circumstances, it was such a good idea to go to the nightclub to see the Thai girl yet again that evening, but he couldn't think of a single valid reason not to.

As always, on his way to the club Mansutti mulled over what he could do with the girl that evening. He was the methodical type and didn't like to improvise. The prospect excited him almost at once and not even the dense white fog could distract him from his thoughts.

On reaching the Bulli & Pupe nightclub, he went to the toilets to spruce himself up a bit, comb his hair and spray on a bit of deodorant. The girl, whose name he hadn't yet learned, was waiting for him, perched on a barstool, sipping fruit juice. As far as she was concerned, Mansutti was no weirder than the others. He was one of many. She watched him walk towards her, grinning broadly, his eyes riveted on her thighs. The hostess could have placed a bet that this evening he would want to bury his nose in her armpit while she gave him a hand-job. It was a while since he had asked for that one.

It was just as she had thought, and an hour or so later Mansutti walked out of the club satisfied and slightly tipsy. He had drunk more than usual, in an attempt to stop himself thinking about the investigation at work that threatened to mess things up for him. He got into his car, a Fiat Bravo he hadn't yet finished paying for. He waited for it to warm up and for the film of ice on his windscreen to melt. He would have liked another cigarette but had sworn not to smoke inside the car, not wanting it to smell like an ashtray.

The corporal was relieved to see that the freezing cold had dispersed the fog. He pulled out of the parking lot and took the main road for Treviso. When he reached Ponte di Piave he would turn off for Noventa and then take the autostrada for Venice.

Rossini, who was following him in a Mercedes with German plates stolen from a hotel lot in Pordenone, also knew that route. Rossini drove along, fidgeting incessantly with his bracelets. He would have just one opportunity to eliminate the corporal. And it would only work if that stretch of road was completely deserted. Nobody should ever suspect that it was anything but an accident. After a gentle bend, there was a long, straight section of road, lined on either side by huge trees. Rossini scoured the darkness up ahead for oncoming headlights, then floored the accelerator. He drew alongside Mansutti's Fiat, forcing it towards the edge of the road. The corporal hit his horn and started gesticulating confusedly. Rossini switched on his inside light so Mansutti could recognize him. He didn't like killing if his victims couldn't look him in the face. It struck him as cowardly and underhand. Mansutti recognized him and was seized with panic. The Mercedes suddenly darted out in front. To avoid hitting it, Mansutti swerved hard and crashed straight into the trunk of a plane tree. Rossini braked hard then reversed back. Mansutti was badly injured but he wasn't dead. The safety belt had seen to that. The old gangster sighed, then took Mansutti's head by the hair and smashed it hard against the steering wheel until he was certain the prison cop was dead.

The news of the fatal accident filled a few lines in the local paper. At the prison, the corporal's colleagues drew lots to decide who should serve as official pall-bearers. Even the collection for the man's separated widow was decidedly meagre. Nobody had ever much liked Vincenzo Mansutti.

Max's plan to blackmail the cops into negotiating with us relied on an element of surprise. And when Stefano Giaroli, late one night, opened the door of his apartment to find three masked men facing him, one of whom was armed with a twenty-two-calibre Ruger fitted with a silencer, he was momentarily speechless.

'Don't even think of playing the hero,' Rossini advised, removing Giaroli's police-issue handgun from his underarm holster.

Max motioned Giaroli towards the only armchair in the apartment. 'Sit down, Marshal. We need to talk.'

Giaroli did what he was told. He took a good look at us, without saying a word. A skillful cop, he was trying to pick up some detail that would help him identify us. Then he reached for his cigarettes. 'If you were going to kill me, you wouldn't have bothered with the balaclavas. So what are you after?'

Max took a chair and sat down opposite him. 'We know all about the special operation to dismantle the super-ecstasy ring, involving Silvestrin, Boscaro, Kupreskic, your corrupt colleague, and the school caretaker. We also know where the drugs factory is located.' Max had deliberately omitted to mention Celegato, not wanting to give Giaroli any clues as to what had led us to our discoveries.

Giaroli inhaled the smoke rather nervously. 'Are you part of the same organization?'

That made the three of us chuckle. 'No, we're not. That's not our line of business,' I assured him.

'So what the fuck are you after?'

'Tone down the attitude, pig,' Rossini warned.

'We haven't yet reconstructed every detail of your operation,' Max lied, 'but it appears your investigation was triggered by the arrest of a Colombian drugs trafficker, one Guillermo Arías Cuevas, who was arrested on his way through Venice airport with a considerable quantity of cocaine in his stomach. Then, in the euphoria of the moment, you inadvertently arrested someone who had nothing whatever to do with the organization you are seeking to dismantle, accusing him of being the Colombian's accomplice. We would like to see the innocence of the party in question recognized, otherwise . . .'

'Otherwise?' Giaroli challenged.

'Otherwise we'll have no choice but to expose and demolish the entire operation.'

'You guys have got to be crazy.'

Max heaved a sigh. 'That may well be. But we still want an answer.'

Giaroli finished his cigarette. 'I'll try to make things clear for you. I don't know who you are, but you talk like a lawyer and could even be a consigliere to the mob,' he said, addressing Max. 'Be that as it may, sooner or later I'll find out who you are and throw you all into jail because no one, I repeat no one, can get away with forcing their way into the home of a member of the Guardia di Finanza, threatening him with a firearm, and blackmailing him. My answer is as follows: Corradi is fine where he is. While it's true he has fuck-all to do with drugs peddling, he does have a little debt outstanding to the police force for the killing of two patrolmen, and it's a debt he is going to have to pay. You can be quite sure that when it comes to trial the judges won't look favorably on him. He'll be lucky if he gets out of prison alive.'

'I get the impression you don't have the slightest intention of negotiating,' Max said, using his friendliest tone of voice.

'Negotiating? You can go fuck yourselves. And stay away from the operation we're conducting or you'll be looking at something much worse than prison.'

'You've got balls, pig,' Rossini said, in a flattering tone of voice. 'But you're making a mistake if you think all you have to do to change our minds is play the hard man. We made you a fair proposal, you turned us down, and now you're going to have to wave bye-bye to this special operation you're so crazy about.'

Giaroli shook his head. 'You're not going to do anything.' Max played our last card. 'It's not just the Guardia di Finanza's special anti-narcotics unit that's involved here. It's a joint operation involving the police. Are you quite sure you're authorized to take this kind of decision? Don't you think it might be an idea to consult your superiors?'

'You can rest assured that the only consultation necessary will focus on precisely how much in the way of extra resources we should devote to discovering your identities.'

Max shrugged. The conversation was over. Beniamino took from his pocket a small bottle and chucked it at Giaroli.

'Drink that dry. It'll put you to sleep till tomorrow morning.' Giaroli couldn't make up his mind whether or not to unscrew the cap. 'Drink it down, pig,' Rossini said. 'Don't force me to shoot you in the knee.'

He knocked the sleeping draught back in a single gulp.

'Now get the fuck out of here, you bastards,' he whispered, collapsing in the armchair.

Negotiation had proved a failure. We now had to demonstrate that our attempt at blackmail wasn't an empty bluff by a bunch of amateurs. We spent an entire night discussing the best way to sabotage the special operation. My proposal was to bring in the media. We could send an envelope containing pictures of the Brenta Mafia mobsters in the company of the

Croatian chemist, along with a page of detailed information, to the main dailies, weeklies and TV newsrooms. My associates felt it wouldn't do the trick.

'Basically, a special operation is a secret investigation conducted by a clandestine body unknown even to the law enforcement agencies,' Max explained patiently. 'To leak information to journalists would mean getting tangled up in a maze of claims and counterclaims. What we need to do is create an event that compels the police and the Finanza to proceed with arrests on the basis of the evidence already gathered. The press will come in at a later stage, by which time we'll have landed the cops in the shit and had Celegato arrested. It would throw everything out of kilter and might just work in Corradi's favor.'

'What precisely do you mean by "create an event"?' I asked, feigning indifference but with one eye on the handgun Rossini had placed on the table. It was the one he had taken off Giaroli.

'Like using a cop's handgun to take out some piece of shit, making sure the weapon is found at the scene of the crime.'

It was one hell of a plan. The murder investigation would quickly trace the gun back to the officer and would demand all manner of explanations, above all how on earth the gun wound up in the possession of a killer. Such an event would be viewed with exceptional gravity. Also, it would be on the lips of every cop and every investigating magistrate in the land. The special operation would no longer be secret and therefore no longer viable.

'They'll hunt us down,' I objected.

'They don't have the faintest idea who they're looking for,' Rossini replied.

'They'll put Corradi's balls in a vice,' I insisted.

'He'll never talk.'

'Maybe not today. But what about tomorrow? Prison drags

and every new day brings fresh temptation. Solving a murder is a great way of getting out.'

'He'll never talk,' Old Rossini repeated wearily.

Two days later I found myself driving a Ford Focus, stolen a few hours previously in Mestre, along the main road to Trieste. Beside me sat Beniamino. We were both wearing latex gloves and my associate was holding Giaroli's 9mm. Beretta between his legs. Max was a couple of kilometers ahead of us in my Skoda. We stopped off in the poorly lit car-park of a shopping mall outside San Donà di Piave, where Rossini stole a couple of car plates, switching them with those of the Focus.

When we reached Trieste, it was almost time for dinner. Max, with the city plan spread out on the seat next to him, led the way to Via Nicolò degli Aldegardi. At number four, on the second floor of an elegant apartment block, lived Vlatko Kupreskic's Italian lover. According to the information we had received, Kupreskic visited her three times a week—Mondays, Wednesdays, and Thursdays. He arrived at about nine in the evening and left early the following morning. It was a Wednesday evening when we turned up.

Max left for home in my Skoda. We parked the Ford just a few meters from the gate. The street was quiet. Apart from a girl out walking her dog, we didn't see a living soul. It was now dinnertime and far too cold anyway to want to go out for a stroll. The Croatian chemist arrived punctually. He stopped his BMW just behind us. Rossini waited until he had walked past our bonnet, then got out.

'Vlatko Kupreskic,' he called out, in a strong, clear voice. The man turned around. Rossini pointed the gun at his heart and pulled the trigger. Kupreskic dropped to the ground without a murmur. Beniamino placed Marshal Giaroli's police-issue handgun on the man's bespattered chest.

We left, tires screeching, but after a couple of hundred meters reduced our speed so as not to attract the attention of any passing police cars. We left the Ford in a lot near the station, immediately getting rid of the parking ticket to eliminate any possible link with the car used for the murder.

The Intercity train for Milan was waiting at the platform. We punched the first-class tickets I had bought that morning at Padova's central station. The second-class carriages were full of Serbs and Romanies arriving in Italy in search of work and fortune. As always, it was on them that the railway police would focus their attention. The first-class carriages, on the other hand, were almost deserted. We sat down facing one another. I kept glancing at my watch but the minutehand seemed frozen. Rossini lit a couple of cigarettes and stuck one of them in my mouth.

'Relax, Marco. The police's quick-response team and the Carabinieri will be along to check out the station in about an hour at the earliest. We know how they work.'

'How do you feel?' I asked.

'I've just killed a chemist who made his fortune refining heroin and manufacturing super-ecstasy. I'd say it was a day well spent.'

'I feel uneasy.'

'Do you know what your problem is, Marco?'

'Out of all those you know about?' I tried to joke.

'You haven't yet understood that things have changed. If you want to continue in this line of work, taking on cases involving the criminal underworld, you're going to have to get used to the idea of playing dirty, bending the rules. All the time, systematically.'

'We've bent the rules before,' I replied.

'Sure. But on all previous occasions, we did it to save our skins. This time it was a matter of choice.'

'Declaring war on the cops is pure madness.'

'It would have been once, when there were precise rules to follow, but things are different now. With the arrival in Italy of all the foreign-based syndicates, the underworld has changed, and the cops and magistrates have changed too. They don't play by the old rules anymore.'

The station-master blew his whistle and the train moved off. We travelled in silence, smoking and peering out at the night. We got off the train at Mestre, picked up Rossini's car and drove to join Max, who was eager to hear how things had gone.

We found him sitting in front of his computer. He looked up at us. 'Everything all right?'

'As smooth as oil,' Rossini replied.

'Then all we have to do now is sit back and watch.'

The next day, the evening news bulletins all devoted a great deal of space to a decisive swoop by the joint forces of the Guardia di Finanza and the police who, according to the reports, had succeeded in rooting out a criminal organization that had been manufacturing and retailing super-ecstasy. The twelve arrests included those of a Guardia di Finanza marshal and his wife, stopped as they were driving at high speed away from their home. In the trunk of their car were found twenty-eight small cellophane bags, containing a total of thirty thousand tablets of a synthetic drug. All the other people arrested resided in Rome. According to the investigators, the drugs were bound for the capital's discotheques and nightclubs.

Something had gone wrong, but we had to wait till the following morning to read the local newspapers, which ran more detailed reports. Rossini woke me up, tossing a paper on my bed. Most of the front page was given over to the story.

EXPOSED. THE DOUBLE LIFE OF
DRUG-DEALING FINANZA OFFICER
Arrested in possession of thirty thousand ecstasy tablets,

a respectable couple beyond suspicion: she was employed as a primary school janitor, he as a marshal in the Guardia di Finanza.

I read every single article, even the interview with the mayor of Tricesimo and the head of the village's municipal police force. There wasn't the slightest hint of any arrests in the Veneto region, nor any mention of Ennio Silvestrin, Alcide Boscaro or Bruno Celegato. Furthermore, the murder of Vlatko Kupreskic was covered in another section of the paper and no link was made with the police and Finanza drugs swoop. The Carabinieri, charged with the investigation into the murder of Kupreskic, stated that they suspected score-settling within the emerging Croatian underworld.

I got up. 'What's going on?'

Beniamino shook his head. 'I don't know. Max is sifting through the papers, but they've all got the same story.'

I pulled on my trousers and a fleece and followed Rossini into Max's apartment. Max was scrolling through the papers on the internet, dunking one biscuit after another into his cappuccino. I wasn't fully awake yet. I grabbed a cup in the kitchen and poured out equal amounts of coffee and Calvados.

'They've fucked us, right?' I asked.

'Good and proper,' Max replied. 'They've kept Celegato and the old-timers from the Brenta Mafia well out of it, and instead have pulled in the Roman branch of the organization headed by Raffaele Bonavita, the drug-peddling Guardia di Finanza marshal.'

'And they've also taken care not to suggest any link between the drugs gang and the late lamented Kupreskic,' Rossini added.

Max nibbled at another biscuit. 'Evidently the special operation was a lot broader than we thought. It may well have consisted of two or more distinct lines of enquiry. Celegato must have infiltrated the gang's nucleus, so to avoid irreparably compromising the entire investigation they decided not to arrest him.'

'Giaroli realized we had only found out about half of their operation, doubtless the less important half,' Rossini remarked.

I finished my coffee. 'So what do we do now?'

'We try to work out why they left Bruno Celegato out of the net,' Max replied.

'I don't think it would be a great idea to start tailing Celegato all over again. If Giaroli suspects it was Celegato who led us to the Corno di Rosazzo drugs factory, we'll walk straight into a trap.'

Max lit his first cigarette of the day. 'That's not going to happen. We'll focus our attention on Silvestrin and Boscaro, the Brenta Mafia old-timers. They've got to occupy pretty key positions within the organization.' He turned to Beniamino.

'You should find out whatever you can about the two of them.'

'That won't be a problem. I know the right people. We should be able to get a line on them by this evening.'

I got up. 'Well, in the meantime, I'm going back to bed.' Old Rossini took hold of my arm. 'What's wrong, Marco?'

'I'm sleepy and I'm pissed. We could have gotten the same results by simply bringing in the press, as I suggested from the start.'

'I don't agree,' Max hit back. 'They've been forced to shut down a part of their investigation and they now have a clearer idea of what we're after. There's still a chance of cutting a deal with them.'

'In my opinion, there was never the slightest hope of that.'

'Listen, Marco. It's not as if we had any choice in the matter. Either Corradi changes his mind and lets his lawyer drag Celegato through the courts, or we have to keep on busting the cops' balls till they make up their minds to negotiate.'

I didn't want to discuss it any further. I waved a hand at my associates and headed back to bed.

Beniamino returned to Max's apartment late that afternoon. He had a smart new haircut and his moustache was trimmed to perfection. He was in an exceptionally good mood.

He poured himself the usual wheat vodka. 'I've had a couple of interesting chats. I dropped in to see Adriana, a working girl from Mestre who used to be Boscaro's lover, when she was still young and beautiful. For three hundred thousand lire, she told me that Alcide has gone back to dope-peddling big-time. He told her so himself. It seems he pops around sometimes for a little servicing, just for old time's sake. It would also appear that Adriana, in the course of her work, has seen him in the company of a number of Venetian crooks. She mentioned three or four names to me, including that of Antonio De Toni, better known as "Toni Baeta," the guy who runs a barber's shop in Venice, right near Piazzale Roma . . .'

The name rang a bell. 'Isn't that the guy you helped escape from Parenzo, three or four years back?'

'That's the one. He tried to rip off some Croats with cocaine that was ninety per cent adulterated and they failed to see the funny side. Anyway, I went to ask him for a favor in return and, going on what he told me, there are a number of drug-dealers—Italians, all of them—most of whom were once members of the old Brenta Mafia, who have now set up a new organization consisting of three or four different gangs. Their aim is to reconquer the Veneto area and take control of the entire market for cocaine and ecstasy.'

'Poor dumb fucks,' Max chuckled. 'If they get lucky, Celegato will land them all in prison. If not, the Albanians, Nigerians and Russians will pick them off one by one.'

'Anyway, right now they're busy as hell,' Beniamino continued. 'They're on the lookout for contacts and channels through which to purchase Colombian coke. According to Toni Baeta, yesterday's arrests only hit the tabs side of their business.'

The bottle of Calvados was empty. I went to the drinks cabinet to fetch another. 'That explains why Celegato is so valuable to the cops. It isn't easy to dismantle an organization consisting of several different gangs. For a job like that, you need a very well-connected insider to reconstruct its command and personnel structure, as well as the drugs-purchasing and sales channels.'

'Did Baeta tell you anything else?' Max asked.

'Just that the main men in the organization meet at a trattoria called Da Nane, between the Rialto and Piazza San Marco.'

Max nodded in satisfaction. 'I think we should go and take a look.'

The following day, Max and I caught the train to Venice. Beniamino stayed at home. He was too well known to pass unobserved in the center of the city, especially given that the only way to get around was on foot or by vaporetto. At Venice station we popped into the toilets and re-emerged dressed as tourists: anoraks, mini-rucksacks, woolly hats and cameras slung around our necks. We set off for the Rialto. In Calle dei Fuseri, as we passed in front of the trattoria that Toni Baeta had mentioned to Rossini, we had to quicken our step. Marshal Giaroli was leaning in a nearby doorway in the arms of a girl with long copper-colored hair. And it certainly wasn't his girlfriend. Presumably she was an agent from the police drug squad, there to keep an eye on the restaurant. We walked straight past him but he didn't move a muscle.

Max noticed my sigh of relief. 'Were you worried he'd recognize us?'

'I was a bit. You have a rather distinctive body shape.'

'I'm not the only obese guy in the world,' he retorted, clearly irritated.

We wandered up and down the neighboring streets and

alleyways, noticing a whole series of people who might be undercover cops.

'Let's get out of here, Max. It's too dangerous.'

We tried again the following day, with the same result. After ditching the idea of monitoring the trattoria, we attempted to take up position outside the homes of Silvestrin and Boscaro in Mestre, but the presence of suspect vans forced us to abandon that too. We then returned to Celegato's apartment, where we found a Fiat Tipo parked just outside, containing a couple of young men and displaying on its roof the tell-tale aerial that adorns all unmarked police vehicles. After a week of getting nowhere, we called off our investigation. It was no longer possible to interfere with the operation. The cops had got wise to us.

'We've lost,' Max declared bitterly. 'If Corradi wants to get out of prison, at his trial he'll have to play it by the book. He has no other way out.'

'And one day soon we're going to have to go and see his lawyer and pass on the message,' I said, equally bitterly.

It was a while since I had been to La Cuccia. I noticed at once that there was a new girl waiting at the tables. Rudy motioned me over to the bar.

'How come Virna's not back yet?' I asked.

'That's precisely what I want to talk to you about. She was supposed to be back at work on Monday, after the weekend, but she phoned in to say she's decided to move on. She's working at a sandwich bar in the center of town.'

I waited in silence as Rudy fixed me an Alligator. Then I went and sat at my usual table, listened to the music, drank and smoked. Same as ever. As if nothing had happened. Then I went home and dug around in my collection of blues records, searching for something as sad as I was, to provide a fitting accompaniment to my sense of defeat. 'Damn Right, I've Got

The Blues' by Buddy Guy seemed to fit the bill. I fell asleep halfway through the second track.

Round about midday, I dragged myself out of bed and went next door to Max's flat to fix myself a cup of coffee. The smell of frying onions forced me to drop the idea. 'Virna has given up working at the club,' I said.

'I know.'

'I'll go around and see her one of these days, on the pretext that I'm taking her her last pay-packet.'

'Good idea.'

'Do you really think so?'

'Sure. I reckon you must have a couple of things to clarify.'

'I'll have to come up with something intelligent to say.'

'It would be a good idea. You don't have that many cards left to play.'

'I feel as if I've run right out of arguments. I know what Virna wants from me but I can't give it to her. So far all I've done is play for time. But now she's got me backed up against a wall.'

'Virna is an intelligent and sensitive woman. You're making a mistake if you think you can talk her into coming back to you and then play the old trick of forever putting off confronting your problems till later.'

'Then I'll lose her.'

'It's possible.'

'I miss her.'

'I can imagine.'

'Sex with her was out of this world.'

'I understand what you're saying.'

'I think I love her.'

'Marco.'

'Yes?'

'Cut it out,' Max snapped. 'You're like a moronic teenager.'

Then he placed the bottle of Calvados in front of me. 'Have a drink and pull yourself together.'

'What's going on?' We turned around to see Rossini standing there, as elegant and well turned out as always.

Max sighed. 'Virna has gone to work at another joint and doesn't want to see him anymore . . .'

'Right. So now he's crying like a bullcalf on the shoulder of the first friend he can find. The old, old story,' Rossini said, twisting the knife.

I took hold of the bottle and stood up. 'I know when I'm not wanted.'

'I've got a better idea,' Beniamino said. 'Why don't you go and get dressed? We need to go and see La Tía.'

'Trouble?'

'I don't know. She's been spreading the word on the Colombian hostess scene that she wants to meet us. I guess we should go and see what she wants.'

Doña Rosa had talked Signora Gianna into giving her a couple of easy chairs. We found her comfortably ensconced in one of them, while Aisa applied polish to her fingernails. She greeted us with highly suspect friendliness and a sly smile.

Rossini took a chair and sat down facing her. 'What do you want?'

'To talk business,' she replied, adopting a harsher tone.

'Explain yourself.'

'I need you to tell me something, information that is important to me. In exchange, I have some information I think will be of great interest to you.'

'What do you want to know?' I asked.

'The first time you turned up here, you knew who I was, who Guillermo was, and you even knew Aurelio's nickname, Alacrán. You can only have gotten this information direct from Colombia. Nobody in Italy knew me, not even Celegato was able to connect me to my nephew. In a few days' time, I'll be going home and I don't want any surprises. I want to know who your contact is.'

Rossini and I glanced at one another. La Tía was frightened. She figured that whoever had supplied us with our information knew she was in Italy and might decide to play some kind of trick on her.

'What are you offering us in exchange?'

La Tía scrutinized her nails then, deeming Aisa's handiwork satisfactory, held out the other hand. 'Over the last few weeks, I've met a lot of people. I've spent a long time chatting with Colombian girls who work the clubs and, above all, I've asked the right people the right questions. I've discovered that the man who's in prison accused of being Guillermo's offloader is called Nazzareno Corradi. I've also met Victoria Rodriguez Gomez, his extremely beautiful girlfriend . . .'

'Get to the point,' Rossini cut in.

'Take it easy, hombre, let me tell it my way,' La Tía snarled. Then she resumed calmly. 'I made a couple of phone calls to Bogotá, asking for information about Celegato, and in the end I discovered that a certain somebody has not been telling you the truth.'

'And who might that be?' I asked, trying to appear unconcerned.

'You go first.'

'I do hope this isn't some kind of trick, because if it is . . .' Beniamino hissed.

La Tía stared him out. 'You haven't yet lost your bad habit of threatening me.'

Rossini, in a gesture of utter scorn, raised his hand a fraction, then asked me to do the talking.

'We happen to have some acquaintances among the Colombian guerrillas. It was FARC who passed the information on to us, and the photographs too,' I said.

Doña Rosa sprang to her feet. 'Marxist sons of bitches,' she spluttered. 'If they know I'm in Italy, they'll place someone at the airport to follow me and try to get at Alacrán.'

'It seems your man used to take a great deal of pleasure in cutting the throats of political activists and peasants,' I continued.

'They were all of them guerrilla fighters,' La Tía retorted.

'Sure. Whatever. Now it's your turn.'

Rosa Gonzales regained her composure and sat back down.

'One of the girls that Celegato took with him to Japan is a cousin of Victoria's. That's not all. About a year ago, a girl from Bogotá who had been working in the Jesolo area moved to Milan. Victoria asked her to do her the favor of not cancelling the lease on her apartment in Jesolo. Victoria said she would pay the rent herself and swore the girl to secrecy. The fact is that Señorita Rodriguez Gomez has a love nest. If I were you I'd go and see who she meets there.'

I was so shocked I didn't know how to react. Beniamino went on smoking calmly. 'The address?'

'I don't have it. I obtained this information at the end of a long process of secret-swapping between Colombian girls. But I know how to spot bullshit in a stream of otherwise truthful gossip. This information's reliable.'

'It can't be Celegato,' I said, getting into the car. 'We followed him several nights running and he never met up with her.'

'Sure. But what about during the day?'

I remembered that Victoria had told Max she couldn't stand being alone in the evenings in that empty house and felt the need to wander from club to club. I mentioned this to Rossini who, in the meantime, had recalled another detail.

'Do you remember the first time we went to Corradi's house to talk to her?'

'Yes, I do.'

'At one point, when she was finding it hard to cope with

our questioning, she picked up a framed photograph and clasped it to her bosom. The photo showed Corradi, Victoria and, standing between them, a man who had his arms round both of them.'

'Celegato!'

'Yeah, Celegato. Who's to say which one she was thinking of at that moment?'

'It just doesn't seem possible. I'm inclined to think La Tía is making a mistake or she's told us a lie.'

'I don't think so. It all adds up. For Corradi to walk into the Pensione Zodiaco trap, Victoria had to be unavailable on her cell phone and, what do you know, that evening she was at the Black Baron where there's no signal. I suspect Celegato told her to go there and, well, make herself unobtainable.'

We drove to Ormelle and stopped on a country lane that gave us a good view of Corradi's house. Victoria's Alfa Romeo was parked in the drive. Just after dark we saw her come out to feed the two rottweilers. Beniamino started the car. 'We'll come back in the morning.'

On the way back to Padova, I glanced over at the bracelets on my associate's left wrist. There were two new ones. One was slender with a catch shaped like the head of a serpent; the other was thicker, with a catch consisting of two miniature anchors. The scalps of Mansutti and Kupreskic.

The following morning we saw Victoria leave home at ten. She stopped for breakfast at the main square in Oderzo and then resumed her journey, all the way to San Biagio di Callalta, near Treviso. She drove into the forecourt of a recently built condominium, parking her car alongside Celegato's yellow Saab.

Rossini shifted into reverse and we returned to Padova.

As soon as he saw our faces, Fat Max knew the result of our stakeout. 'She's seeing that rat, isn't she?'

I nodded, still struggling to take it in. 'I'd never have believed it,' Max continued. 'She seemed truly, sincerely, devastated by Nazzareno's arrest.'

'And all the while she was hanging around us, just trying to work out whether we were following the Celegato lead,' I replied.

'They must have been seeing each other for a year or more,' Old Rossini said, thinking aloud. 'Ever since she got hold of that love nest.'

'And as soon as the opportunity presented itself, Bruno leapt at the chance to put his romantic rival out of circulation. Which is why, of all the people he could have sold to the cops, he chose poor old Nazzareno,' I added.

'I don't understand all the secrecy,' Max said. 'Victoria and Corradi weren't even married. They were both perfectly entitled to pack their bags and leave any time they liked.'

'The rules of the criminal underworld,' Rossini explained.

'You don't get involved with a friend's woman. Not even if she leaves him.'

I abstained from any comment. 'This afternoon we had better go and see Bonotto and pass a message on to Nazzareno. He needs to know about Victoria. Maybe this new blow will make him change his mind. Who knows?'

'Sometimes I don't understand you, Marco,' snapped Rossini, getting heated. 'Surely you don't want him to go to the trial and rat, do you?'

I tried to restrain my anger but failed. 'I don't get you either, Beniamino. It's not about ratting. Just tell me why the fuck that poor hapless bastard, a man innocent as charged, should have to grow old behind bars? To save the asses of his woman and his best friend, both of whom have betrayed him? Or to protect cops who took the law into their own hands to fit him up?'

Beniamino smashed his fist down on the table. 'Rules,' he shouted. 'You don't get out of prison by accusing others.'

It was my turn to yell. 'Don't you realize how absurd it is to stick to the rules when drugs are involved?'

'That makes no difference. Even if he was accused of paedophilia, he would still be obliged to remain silent.'

'Calm down, the two of you,' Max broke in, refilling our glasses.

'Answer me this, Marco,' Rossini continued, lowering his voice. 'If you were in Corradi's shoes and you discovered it was Virna and Max who had put you behind bars, would you tell your lawyer to drag them through the courts?'

'No, I wouldn't,' I replied at once. 'But that doesn't mean the rules aren't totally fucked up. In such circumstances, I would feel obliged to comply with them because the alternative would be worse. But if Nazzareno decided to come out fighting in court, I would respect his decision. It wouldn't be for me to sit in judgment over him.'

Max explained to Bonotto that our investigation had run into the sand and that we couldn't help his client any further. Obviously he skipped a number of details, not least the murder of the Croatian chemist. He concluded his report by handing over the photographic material we had collected during the various stakeouts, and the tape of the conversation between Celegato and Rosa Gonzales Cuevas at the Ristorante Barchessa in Caposile.

'This material is more than enough to win the case,' Bonotto said. 'If Corradi would only listen to me.'

'Please tell him that if he decides to follow your advice he'll have my total sympathy.'

'Thank you for that, Buratti. I'll pass it on, without fail. However, I've decided to play a little trick on my client. The preliminary hearing is set for the twenty-fourth of March, and I have decided to place Celegato's name on the list of witnesses to be called. I want Nazzareno to make up his mind what to do while looking his friend in the eye.'

'A waste of time,' Rossini commented.

I handed Bonotto a sealed envelope. 'You should deliver this to Corradi.'

Bonotto handed it straight back. 'I can't do that. As you well know.'

'It relates to Corradi's personal life,' Rossini explained.

The lawyer rested his hands on his desk. 'That makes no difference. I can pass on to him by word of mouth the content of the message and then report back to you his answer, should there be one. I'm bound by professional secrecy, and that ought to be more than enough for you.'

'Okay,' Max said. 'We wish to inform Corradi that for some time now Victoria has been betraying him with Bruno Celegato.'

'What?' Bonotto asked in astonishment. 'That's not possible.'

'We are absolutely certain of it,' Max confirmed.

'To think she kept coming around here begging me to do whatever I could to get Corradi out of prison, playing the inconsolable little woman,' Bonotto continued.

I shrugged. 'She fooled the lot of us.'

'So she was aware of Celegato's activities. Including his role in my client's arrest,' Bonotto went on.

Max lit another cigarette. 'We want to know what Nazzareno intends to do about this.'

Bonotto looked us all hard in the eye. 'Let it be quite clear that I am not a conduit for orders relating to murder or violence of any kind.'

'What on earth are you thinking of?' I said with a laugh.

'Max was referring to a quite different matter—the fact that Victoria is living in his house and spending his money.'

'I apologize, Buratti.'

'Forget it. When are you intending to see him next?'

'Tomorrow morning. I'll call you as soon as I leave the prison.'

At eleven o'clock the next morning I was still sleeping and, in the perennial mess that is my home, it took me a while to locate the phone.

'How did he react?' I asked.

'Not well. He burst into tears and it took me quite some time to calm him down.'

'I'm sorry.'

'What I'm sorry about is the fact that Corradi is still stubbornly refusing to implicate those responsible for his arrest. It's an absurd position to adopt.'

'Has he decided what to do about Victoria?'

'Yes, he has. He asked me to remind you that you promised him you would look after her if things went badly. He would like you to see that she returns to Colombia. Immediately.'

'Okay.'

'Buratti?'

'What?'

'Provided she agrees to go, obviously,' he stressed.

'Obviously, Avvocato. Don't worry.'

Victoria greeted me with her usual shy smile. She smiled at Old Rossini too, but her mouth fell open when she saw La Tía. She touched her hair with an uncertain gesture. 'What's going on?'

'You're going back to Colombia. Today. And for good.'

She backed into the lounge. I picked up the framed photograph of her, Corradi and Celegato laughing, their arms thrown round one another. I pointed at the police informant and she understood. She burst into tears. Doña Rosa walked over to her and stroked her hair. 'Don't cry, chica. From now on, I'll be taking care of you.'

Victoria pulled away and La Tía slapped her violently.

'You're going to be my little whore,' she told her. Then she reached her hand down between Victoria's legs. 'Here I want you rubia, blonde,' she whispered in her ear.

Victoria let out a yell and tried to escape from her grip but La Tía pressed a hairpin against her throat. 'You have family in Colombia. Father, mother, two sisters, baby brother and granny. You want to see them all dead?'

She shook her head and fell to her knees, begging us not to make her leave Italy.

'It's what Nazzareno wants,' Rossini explained. 'You should count yourself lucky you're still alive and that you and your snitch of a boyfriend haven't been thrown in prison.'

I handed her a glass of grappa. She drank it down and somehow found the strength to pull on her coat. Rossini rummaged through her bag and took out her passport and residence permit. As we left the house, the two rottweilers began to bark.

'What'll happen to them?' I asked Beniamino.

'I know a vet in Oderzo. Tomorrow I'll get him to come and fetch them.'

When we got to Mestre we went through a back entrance into a store selling photographic equipment. It belonged to a masterforger, an old acquaintance from our prison days. He sat Victoria down on a stool opposite the polaroid he used for passport photos. He rearranged her hair, used a paper handkerchief to dry her mascara-streaked tears, and took the snap. He then picked up Aisa's and Victoria's passports and switched the photographs. This had been La Tía's idea. She had taken a fancy to Victoria one night when she had met her at a club and when we had suggested she take Victoria back to Colombia with her, she had decided to leave Aisa behind in Italy. Aisa would end up as a hostess. Yet another.

'Aren't you afraid she'll take revenge on you by going to the police and telling them what she knows about your organization?' I had asked her.

'Aisa has a big family in Colombia,' she had replied.

They all had families in Colombia and they were all terrified. Threatening someone's relatives was like reciting a magic spell.

We drove them to the station. I unloaded Doña Rosa's bags onto the pavement. Victoria's face was as white as marble and her eyes stayed fixed on the ground. La Tía took her by the hand and looked at us with a smile.

'You'll forgive me if I don't tell you precisely how and when I'll be arriving in Bogotá, but the fact is I can't trust you. You might be tempted to pass the information on to those Marxist sons of bitches in FARC.'

'You can bet on it,' Rossini scowled. 'I hope they kill you real soon.'

This failed to wipe the smile off Doña Rosa's lips. She summoned a porter and headed for the ticket office. Victoria followed her docilely.

We got back in the car. I wasn't proud of what we had done. Beniamino sensed what was on my mind. 'Don't even think about it, Marco. Right now, it upsets you because she has a face like an angel but has ended up in the power of that snake La Tía. But just remember how she betrayed Corradi and ratted him out to the cops. Victoria is a snitch. She deserves nothing better.'

I turned up the volume on the car stereo. Robben Ford's 'Tired of Talkin' helped me forget Victoria's empty, absent gaze.

A few days later we heard that Bruno Celegato had been to every nightclub in the entire region searching for Victoria. Nobody was able to help him. He repeatedly phoned her relatives in Bogotá, but her father always replied that he had no news of his daughter's whereabouts.

Old Rossini returned to his smuggling activities. Max and I worked on a couple of missing-persons cases: a doctor's wife in the throes of some sort of mystical crisis and an obese, unhappy teenager who had fallen out with his mom. Two dead-end fucking cases.

Every time I went to La Cuccia, I couldn't help but look for Virna, and it made me sad to see her place occupied by the new girl, a young brunette with a ready smile. One evening I plucked up the courage to go and see Virna at the sandwich-bar where she worked, in the centre of the city. She noticed me at once and came over with an icy expression on her face. She asked me to excuse her but she was very busy and couldn't stop to talk. I handed her the envelope containing her last month's wages, then left.

On March 16, the police and the Guardia di Finanza

launched their operation to smash the Veneto drug ring. Beniamino woke me up the following morning waving a copy of the *Gazzettino di Venezia* under my nose.

COCAINE RESTAURANT, 27 ARRESTS

Following orders from the city's investigating magistrates, the historic Trattoria da Nane has been closed down. The chief of police commented, 'Nowhere is safe from drugs anymore, not even the centre of Venice.' The police and the Guardia di Finanza are working to dismantle a major warehousing operation for drugs originating in South America, based in premises situated in Venice's central Calle dei Fuseri. The operation's code name is 'Mozzarella by the kilo.'

Among those arrested I noticed the names of Toni Vassallo and his wife, as well as all those on the list that Beniamino had given La Tía. Rossini was grinning from ear to ear.

'That's the end of La Tía's Italian connection.'

'Celegato has got away clean yet again.'

'Well, what did you expect?'

'In eight days, Nazzareno's case will come up for the preliminary hearing. I wonder what he's decided to do . . .'

Rossini looked at me askance. 'He'll behave like a man.'

Avvocato Bonotto stood up and adjusted his gown. 'Your honour, we would like to call Bruno Celegato.'

Visibly surprised, Corradi gripped the bars separating him from the rest of the courtroom. The usher led Celegato in and, once he had taken the oath, asked him to turn and face the court.

'The defense counsel may proceed,' the judge said.

Bonotto said nothing, turning instead to stare at his client.

'Bruno,' Corradi shouted. 'Look me in the face.'

Celegato didn't move. He had kept his eyes on the floor ever since entering the courtroom.

Nazzareno waited a few seconds, then turned towards Bonotto and shook his head.

'Forgive me, your honor. The defense counsel has decided not to interrogate this witness.'

Celegato, as pale as death, was led out, his head bowed.

'Does the defense wish to call any other witness evidence?'

'No, your honor.'

The trial itself was held a couple of months later. The proceedings lasted two days, at the end of which the defendant was convicted and sentenced to fourteen years' imprisonment.

I heard the outcome of the trial on the evening news, and knocked on Max's door.

'Fourteen years,' I said.

'We did what we could, Marco.'

'I don't know.'

'But we did. It's this country that has lost any sense of where truth lies. Maybe it never had it.'

'Whose side are we on, Max?'

'The side of the innocent.'

'I never really doubted it, but I'm happy to hear you say it.'

That evening I went back to the sandwich-bar to see Virna. She was wearing her hair in a new way and had put on a few kilos. To me she looked incredibly beautiful.

'I miss you, Virna,' I said softly as she brought me a glass of Calvados. I hadn't ordered anything and Calvados wasn't on the list of drinks available. Maybe she had put a bottle aside, waiting for me to come back. In any case, right then, that's what I wanted to believe.

'I miss you,' I repeated. She surveyed me at length, without a word. Then she resumed serving the other tables. I stayed until the place closed, trying not to overdo it with the drink and thinking about what I could possibly do to win her back. I couldn't resign myself to the idea of losing her for ever.

I walked her to her car. 'I'd like to see you again.'

'We could go out one evening for dinner,' she suggested, to my great surprise. 'I want to explain to you why I left.'

'I've got things to say to you, too.'

She caressed my face, then went home alone. Without me. The following day, Beniamino dropped by to see Max and me, bearing caviar and Cuban cigars. 'I had a bit of trouble at sea last night,' he began to relate. 'Two motorboats from the Guardia di Finanza started following me, and when they realized I was losing them, they opened fire with a twenty millimeter light cannon. It's all the fault of those smugglers down in Puglia. Those nuts are prepared to declare open war on the Guardia di Finanza, all for four lousy crates of cigarettes.'

I offered him a glass of his favorite vodka. 'They're not smugglers, those people,' I said. 'They're mafiosi, Southern Italian mobsters with bases all over Montenegro.'

'You're right there, Marco, they're not really smugglers at all. Real smuggling is like cops and robbers. You run and the Finanza runs after you. Whoever runs faster wins. No violence on either side.'

Max prepared a slap-up lunch: yellow pumpkin risotto followed by baccalà alla vicentina. At the end of the meal, Rossini blew the smoke of a Montecristo number five into his glass of cognac. 'I've got news of Celegato.'

'Tell us about it, partner.'

'It appears someone has been spreading rumours about Victoria among Colombian nightclub hostesses. A word here and a word there, with the result that Celegato found out she's gone back home. But the most interesting thing is that a few days ago our dear old friend Bruno confided in Toni Baeta, the barber, that he's planning to make a trip to Colombia in the near future.'

Max guffawed and raised his glass to Rossini. 'I wonder who'd be spreading rumours like that, eh?'

I shook my head. 'If he goes to Bogotá, he's a dead man. If

La Tía's killers don't get him, those in the pay of the prostitution rackets sure as hell will.'

Beniamino picked up the box of cigars, lifted the lid and held it out to me. I chose the lightest in color, ran it under my nose, clipped the end, and lit it with a long wooden match. The spirals of smoke were white and dense. They reminded me of fog. And winter.

Author's note

This book is dedicated to a friend, a dear friend. The story of Nazzareno Corradi is his story. At sixty years of age, though innocent as charged, he is serving a long prison sentence for international narcotics trafficking. He was unwilling to play by the rules of the law, so the name that could have thrown open the prison gates never left his lips. He preferred to remain loyal to his lifelong principles. I am proud of his silence. It wasn't for him to speak, but for justice to do its work.

Having a friend in prison is like having a friend who is dead but who perhaps one day will return from the grave and re-enter your life. While waiting, I have put aside a bottle of 'venerable' Calvados, and in my garden I have planted an oak tree to give him the strength to go on. Small, senseless gestures to keep old nightmares at bay.

Along with a few others, I did what I could to help him. It made no difference. Even though there was no evidence. And even though my friend's rooted aversion to drugs was well known.

We met in jail. We were all 'long-stay' prisoners. Some of us had the words 'RELEASE DATE: NEVER' stamped in red ink on our files. A number of the prisoners in our section had links to the usual lousy mafia-style organizations and had set up a heroin-trafficking ring. Corrupt guards brought the stuff into the prison and these guys peddled it. It was straightforward and lucrative.

We told them we wanted nothing to do with it. For a variety of reasons, drug-dealers and heroin pissed us off. There were three of us: me, my friend, and a guy from Verona who was both a poet and a murderer. It was a rough time. We became friends watching each others' backs at shower time. Two of us would wash while the third stood guard, a bathrobe rolled round his left arm and the handle of a frying-pan, filed to razor sharpness, clasped in his right hand.

In the end we managed to force a negotiation, and everything was resolved by a series of internal transfers. Somebody, however, took the view that we had broken some unwritten law, and the poet from Verona ended up paying for all three of us. One day he said a word too many and thereby wrote his own death sentence. We realized this immediately, and my friend and I have always thought that he did it on purpose. Remorse had already killed him some time earlier. A couple of years later he was released on probation, and then he disappeared. His body was discovered in the Adige river. His wife recognized him from a tattoo on the big toe of his right foot.

If a person's word counted for anything in the courts of Italy, I would have appeared before the judges and told them what happened in prison all those years ago. But it doesn't. So it remains just a story. One of many.

ABOUT THE AUTHOR

Massimo Carlotto is one of the best known living crime writers in Europe. In addition to the many titles in his extremely popular "Alligator" series, and his stand-alone noir novels, he is also the author of *The Fugitive*, in which he tells the story of his arrest and trial for a crime he didn't commit, and his subsequent years on the run. Carlotto's novel *The Goodbye Kiss* was a finalist for the MWA's Edgar Award for Best Novel.

NOW AVAILABLE FROM EUROPA EDITIONS
(alphabetical by author)

Fiction

Carmine Abate
Between Two Seas • 978-1-933372-40-2 • Territories: World
The Homecoming Party • 978-1-933372-83-9 • Territories: World

Milena Agus
From the Land of the Moon • 978-1-60945-001-4 • Ebook • Territories:
World (excl. ANZ)

Salwa Al Neimi
The Proof of the Honey • 978-1-933372-68-6 • Ebook • Territories: World
(excl UK)

Simonetta Agnello Hornby
The Nun • 978-1-60945-062-5 • Territories: World

Daniel Arsand
Lovers • 978-1-60945-071-7 • Ebook • Territories: World

Jenn Ashworth
A Kind of Intimacy • 978-1-933372-86-0 • Territories: US & Can

Beryl Bainbridge
The Girl in the Polka Dot Dress • 978-1-60945-056-4 • Ebook •
Territories: US

Muriel Barbery
The Elegance of the Hedgehog • 978-1-933372-60-0 • Ebook • Territories:
World (excl. UK & EU)
Gourmet Rhapsody • 978-1-933372-95-2 • Ebook • Territories: World
(excl. UK & EU)

Stefano Benni
Margherita Dolce Vita • 978-1-933372-20-4 • Territories: World
Timeskipper • 978-1-933372-44-0 • Territories: World

Romano Bilenchi
The Chill • 978-1-933372-90-7 • Territories: World

Kazimierz Brandys
Rondo • 978-1-60945-004-5 • Territories: World

Alina Bronsky
Broken Glass Park • 978-1-933372-96-9 • Ebook • Territories: World
The Hottest Dishes of the Tartar Cuisine • 978-1-60945-006-9 • Ebook •
Territories: World

Jesse Browner
Everything Happens Today • 978-1-60945-051-9 • Ebook • Territories:
World (excl. UK & EU)

Francisco Coloane
Tierra del Fuego • 978-1-933372-63-1 • Ebook • Territories: World

Rebecca Connell
The Art of Losing • 978-1-933372-78-5 • Territories: US

Laurence Cossé
A Novel Bookstore • 978-1-933372-82-2 • Ebook • Territories: World
An Accident in August • 978-1-60945-049-6 • Territories: World (excl. UK)

Diego De Silva
I Hadn't Understood • 978-1-60945-065-6 • Territories: World

Shashi Deshpande
The Dark Holds No Terrors • 978-1-933372-67-9 • Territories: US

Steve Erickson
Zeroville • 978-1-933372-39-6 • Territories: US & Can
These Dreams of You • 978-1-60945-063-2 • Territories: US & Can

Elena Ferrante
The Days of Abandonment • 978-1-933372-00-6 • Ebook • Territories: World
Troubling Love • 978-1-933372-16-7 • Territories: World
The Lost Daughter • 978-1-933372-42-6 • Territories: World

Linda Ferri
Cecilia • 978-1-933372-87-7 • Territories: World

Damon Galgut
In a Strange Room • 978-1-60945-011-3 • Ebook • Territories: USA

Santiago Gamboa
Necropolis • 978-1-60945-073-1 • Ebook • Territories: World

Jane Gardam
Old Filth • 978-1-933372-13-6 • Ebook • Territories: US
The Queen of the Tambourine • 978-1-933372-36-5 • Ebook • Territories: US
The People on Privilege Hill • 978-1-933372-56-3 • Ebook • Territories: US
The Man in the Wooden Hat • 978-1-933372-89-1 • Ebook • Territories: US
God on the Rocks • 978-1-933372-76-1 • Ebook • Territories: US
Crusoe's Daughter • 978-1-60945-069-4 • Ebook • Territories: US

Anna Gavalda
French Leave • 978-1-60945-005-2 • Ebook • Territories: US & Can

Seth Greenland
The Angry Buddhist • 978-1-60945-068-7 • Ebook • Territories: World

Katharina Hacker
The Have-Nots • 978-1-933372-41-9 • Territories: World (excl. India)

Patrick Hamilton
Hangover Square • 978-1-933372-06-8 • Territories: US & Can

James Hamilton-Paterson
Cooking with Fernet Branca • 978-1-933372-01-3 • Territories: US
Amazing Disgrace • 978-1-933372-19-8 • Territories: US
Rancid Pansies • 978-1-933372-62-4 • Territories: USA

Alfred Hayes
The Girl on the Via Flaminia • 978-1-933372-24-2 • Ebook •
Territories: World

Jean-Claude Izzo
The Lost Sailors • 978-1-933372-35-8 • Territories: World
A Sun for the Dying • 978-1-933372-59-4 • Territories: World

Gail Jones
Sorry • 978-1-933372-55-6 • Territories: US & Can

Ioanna Karystiani
The Jasmine Isle • 978-1-933372-10-5 • Territories: World
Swell • 978-1-933372-98-3 • Territories: World

Peter Kocan
Fresh Fields • 978-1-933372-29-7 • Territories: US, EU & Can
The Treatment and the Cure • 978-1-933372-45-7 • Territories: US, EU & Can

Helmut Krausser
Eros • 978-1-933372-58-7 • Territories: World

Amara Lakhous
Clash of Civilizations Over an Elevator in Piazza Vittorio •
978-1-933372-61-7 • Ebook • Territories: World
Divorce Islamic Style • 978-1-60945-066-3 • Ebook • Territories: World

Lia Levi
The Jewish Husband • 978-1-933372-93-8 • Territories: World

Valerio Massimo Manfredi
The Ides of March • 978-1-933372-99-0 • Territories: US

Leïla Marouane
The Sexual Life of an Islamist in Paris • 978-1-933372-85-3 •
Territories: World

Lorenzo Mediano
The Frost on His Shoulders • 978-1-60945-072-4 • Ebook •
Territories: World

Sélim Nassib
I Loved You for Your Voice • 978-1-933372-07-5 • Territories: World
The Palestinian Lover • 978-1-933372-23-5 • Territories: World

Amélie Nothomb
Tokyo Fiancée • 978-1-933372-64-8 • Territories: US & Can
Hygiene and the Assassin • 978-1-933372-77-8 • Ebook • Territories: US & Can

Valeria Parrella
For Grace Received • 978-1-933372-94-5 • Territories: World

Alessandro Piperno
The Worst Intentions • 978-1-933372-33-4 • Territories: World
Persecution • 978-1-60945-074-8 • Ebook • Territories: World

Lorcan Roche
The Companion • 978-1-933372-84-6 • Territories: World

Boualem Sansal
The German Mujahid • 978-1-933372-92-1 • Ebook • Territories: US & Can

Eric-Emmanuel Schmitt
The Most Beautiful Book in the World • 978-1-933372-74-7 • Ebook •
Territories: World
The Woman with the Bouquet • 978-1-933372-81-5 • Ebook • Territories:
US & Can

Angelika Schrobsdorff
You Are Not Like Other Mothers • 978-1-60945-075-5 • Ebook •
Territories: World

Audrey Schulman
Three Weeks in December • 978-1-60945-064-9 • Ebook • Territories: US
& Can

James Scudamore
Heliopolis • 978-1-933372-73-0 • Ebook • Territories: US

Luis Sepúlveda
The Shadow of What We Were • 978-1-60945-002-1 • Ebook • Territories:
World

Paolo Sorrentino
Everybody's Right • 978-1-60945-052-6 • Ebook • Territories: US & Can

Domenico Starnone
First Execution • 978-1-933372-66-2 • Territories: World

Henry Sutton
Get Me out of Here • 978-1-60945-007-6 • Ebook • Territories: US & Can

Chad Taylor
Departure Lounge • 978-1-933372-09-9 • Territories: US, EU & Can

Roma Tearne
Mosquito • 978-1-933372-57-0 • Territories: US & Can
Bone China • 978-1-933372-75-4 • Territories: US

André Carl van der Merwe
Moffie • 978-1-60945-050-2 • Ebook • Territories: World
(excl. S. Africa)

Fay Weldon
Chalcot Crescent • 978-1-933372-79-2 • Territories: US

Anne Wiazemsky
My Berlin Child • 978-1-60945-003-8 • Territories: US & Can

Jonathan Yardley
Second Reading • 978-1-60945-008-3 • Ebook • Territories: US & Can

Edwin M. Yoder Jr.
Lions at Lamb House • 978-1-933372-34-1 • Territories: World

Michele Zackheim
Broken Colors • 978-1-933372-37-2 • Territories: World

Alice Zeniter
Take This Man • 978-1-60945-053-3 • Territories: World

Tonga Books

Ian Holding
Of Beasts and Beings • 978-1-60945-054-0 • Ebook • Territories: US & Can

Sara Levine
Treasure Island!!! • 978-0-14043-768-3 • Ebook • Territories: World

www.europaeditions.com

Alexander Maksik
You Deserve Nothing • 978-1-60945-048-9 • Ebook • Territories: US, Can & EU (excl. UK)

Thad Ziolkowski
Wichita • 978-1-60945-070-0 • Ebook • Territories: World

Europa World Noir

Massimo Carlotto
The Goodbye Kiss • 978-1-933372-05-1 • Ebook • Territories: World
Death's Dark Abyss • 978-1-933372-18-1 • Ebook • Territories: World
The Fugitive • 978-1-933372-25-9 • Ebook • Territories: World
Bandit Love • 978-1-933372-80-8 • Ebook • Territories: World
Poisonville • 978-1-933372-91-4 • Ebook • Territories: World

Giancarlo De Cataldo
The Father and the Foreigner • 978-1-933372-72-3 • Territories: World

Caryl Férey
Zulu • 978-1-933372-88-4 • Ebook • Territories: World (excl. UK & EU)
Utu • 978-1-60945-055-7 • Ebook • Territories: World (excl. UK & EU)

Alicia Giménez-Bartlett
Dog Day • 978-1-933372-14-3 • Territories: US & Can
Prime Time Suspect • 978-1-933372-31-0 • Territories: US & Can
Death Rites • 978-1-933372-54-9 • Territories: US & Can

Jean-Claude Izzo
Total Chaos • 978-1-933372-04-4 • Territories: US & Can
Chourmo • 978-1-933372-17-4 • Territories: US & Can
Solea • 978-1-933372-30-3 • Territories: US & Can

Matthew F. Jones
Boot Tracks • 978-1-933372-11-2 • Territories: US & Can

Gene Kerrigan
The Midnight Choir • 978-1-933372-26-6 • Territories: US & Can
Little Criminals • 978-1-933372-43-3 • Territories: US & Can

Carlo Lucarelli
Carte Blanche • 978-1-933372-15-0 • Territories: World
The Damned Season • 978-1-933372-27-3 • Territories: World
Via delle Oche • 978-1-933372-53-2 • Territories: World

Edna Mazya
Love Burns • 978-1-933372-08-2 • Territories: World (excl. ANZ)

Yishai Sarid
Limassol • 978-1-60945-000-7 • Ebook • Territories: World (excl. UK, AUS & India)

Joel Stone
The Jerusalem File • 978-1-933372-65-5 • Ebook • Territories: World

Benjamin Tammuz
Minotaur • 978-1-933372-02-0 • Ebook • Territories: World

Non-fiction

Alberto Angela
A Day in the Life of Ancient Rome • 978-1-933372-71-6 • Territories: World • History

Helmut Dubiel
Deep In the Brain: Living with Parkinson's Disease • 978-1-933372-70-9 •
Ebook • Territories: World • Medicine/Memoir

James Hamilton-Paterson
Seven-Tenths: The Sea and Its Thresholds • 978-1-933372-69-3 • Territories:
USA • Nature/Essays

Daniele Mastrogiacomo
Days of Fear • 978-1-933372-97-6 • Ebook • Territories: World • Current
affairs/Memoir/Afghanistan/Journalism

Valery Panyushkin
Twelve Who Don't Agree • 978-1-60945-010-6 • Ebook • Territories:
World • Current affairs/Memoir/Russia/Journalism

Christa Wolf
One Day a Year: 1960-2000 • 978-1-933372-22-8 • Territories: World •
Memoir/History/20th Century

Children's Illustrated Fiction

Altan
Here Comes Timpa • 978-1-933372-28-0 • Territories: World (excl. Italy)
Timpa Goes to the Sea • 978-1-933372-32-7 • Territories: World (excl. Italy)
Fairy Tale Timpa • 978-1-933372-38-9 • Territories: World (excl. Italy)

Wolf Erlbruch
The Big Question • 978-1-933372-03-7 • Territories: US & Can
The Miracle of the Bears • 978-1-933372-21-1 • Territories: US & Can
(with **Gioconda Belli**) *The Butterfly Workshop* • 978-1-933372-12-9 •
Territories: US & Can